The Hated Ones

by Mike Fiorito

BORDIGHERA PRESS

Cover art by Pat Singer.

Library of Congress Cataloging-in-Publication Data

Names: Fiorito, Mike, author.
Title: The Hated Ones / by Mike Fiorito.
Description: New York, NY : Bordighera Press, [2021] | Series: VIA folios ; 153 | Summary: "Mike Fiorito shoots the brief documentary tales of "The Hated Ones" in a vivid black and white, bringing to life a "Basketball Diaries"-like world of ne'er-do-wells growing up on the wrong side of whatever tracks separate the silver spoons from the rest of us with our wayward fathers, disappointed mothers, and ill-defined dreams of being somebody"-- Provided by publisher.
Identifiers: LCCN 2021018984 | ISBN 9781599541747 (paperback)
Subjects: LCSH: Italian-Americans--New York (State)--New York--Fiction. | LCGFT: Short stories.
Classification: LCC PS3606.I68 H38 2021 | DDC 813/.6--dc23
LC record available at https://lccn.loc.gov/2021018984

Printed in the United States.

Published by
BORDIGHERA PRESS
John D. Calandra Italian American Institute
25 W. 43rd Street, 17th Floor
New York, NY 10036

VIA Folios 153
ISBN 978-1-59954-174-7

The Hated Ones

VIA Folios 153

TABLE OF CONTENTS

To Mom

Here's much to do with hate, but more with love.

WILLIAM SHAKESPEARE

FOREWORD

Heat drives these stories. From the inner heat that pumps torque to our primal urges, to the oppression of sunshine that only growing up in poverty and deprivation knows. Heat from which there is no relief and the unaware teen only makes it worse seeking escape with psychedelic tripsters. Vinny, a third-generation Sicilian New York baby boomer, hand holds us through his world in this collection of interlaced stories that weave like a new shoelace in and out of the rivets up a sneaker. Every walk home is a path of fist fights. Fists speak and hold heat. Every walk out of the apartment is in pursuit of a girl, a high, or music. Vinny's insights are peppered throughout the book. "Junk makes a person no longer themselves. They don't know who you are, or only remember you as if from a dream." The corner is the locus of belonging. Vinny stands with the gang, on the corner, not in the gang but with the gang. Readers who grew up in the boroughs will recognize their brothers or themselves in his exploits, innermost urges, and terror. "I wait for the bullet to come at me and punch me into another realm." If you ever wondered where your mother's one good ring went, or where your brother disappeared to, the answers and your instinctual suspicions are confirmed in these pages.

The setting of Vinny's upbringing is the Ravenswood Houses, forty acres of projects in the northwest part of Queens—Astoria. Seven-story brick buildings with squares of green space and trees, dark corners and pockets, quiet stairwells that lead to rooftops where Manhattan beams at sunset with all the promise of the city on the hill, Oz, the place of dreams and destinations if only one can get out of the projects alive. Vinny's bedroom window is three stories up, overlooking a Department of Sanitation depot and a park with a cement ground and cement walls. Underneath the cement, he tells us, is an African burial ground. His narrative meditations recount stories of torture and beheadings; lynchings of African Americans in early New York. Herein lies the seed of the artist's budding consciousness. Salvation is an obstacle course where he belly crawls back into the shade of the nearest cave—a friend's room, because he is lucky. White. Cute. With a jewel blue-eyed unassuming anti-hero everyman magnetism that gets him girls, jobs, a leg up just when the bottom is about to fall out. "I could smash a bottle and walk away uninjured. I was made of glass; the bottle would become a part of me, dissolve into my being." Vinny is lucky. Race privileged. Gender privileged. For him, birds tweet in rock ballads blasted out project windows. His ancestors transport him into a future as a "good man" via magical Moog synthesizers, Hammond organs and Mellotrons. Jesus hangs on the cross in every moment, witnessing him in the pit of sexual abuse and at the apex of sexual adventure. Jesus is there. Shakespeare is *capeeshed* in gangster-ese. Education is a four-letter word. The verb "to study" is a curse. Dreams become bursts of glass shredding skin into ablutions of blood on the pavement. Concrete bleeds. Skin is concrete. Innocence is shattered at every opportunity. The safest places turn out to be the most unsafe. To be taken under the wing of a mentor becomes the source of dissociations and trauma for a lifetime. And the unsafe places, the places a sober attentive parent would never allow their children to roam, become the sole launchpads for the soul's ambition.

What happens to the children who never hop rooftop fences or ride the wind between subway cars or yank the whammy bar of an electric guitar? The children who don't dare find alternative escape routes up and over adjacent rooftops and down fire escapes and staircases? What happens to children left behind in a world of white privilege even for poor whites? What happens to the boys of color who are passed over when mediocre and high white boys get ushered past them on long sidewalk queues into jobs, even as scabs, but paychecks nonetheless? Prison, death await. Maybe redemption. Maybe tomorrows. Maybe.

Vinny is not one of the children the sky leaves behind. Vinny climbs. Author Mike Fiorito wrote this book as a portrait of the artist as a young man. As in all of his *oeuvre* especially *Call Me Guido* (Ovunque Siamo Press), Fiorito's learning how to play music and how to listen to music, stokes his enlightenment and appreciation for generations past. The paving stones that make the path forward up and out for Vinny are the epic rock albums of the 70's on which he can land. They ultimately lead him to Mozart and Vivaldi. A white Stratocaster becomes his Pegasus offering ascension into tomorrow. These pages make it clear that the children who make it up and out, who get the jobs and the scholarships, are not pole-vaulting themselves over intergenerational poverty, trauma, and depression through a function of their skillsets, effort or ability, rather are prone to the lottery of luck: race, gender, class, and the singular ratchet set of the adults around them—relative sobriety, gambler-holicness, violence, rage, and who they take it out on. This book leaves you counting your blessings. Each and every one. Most poignantly the moments you were angelically snagged out of the abyss. "One hand holding him from death." "None of his tags remain."

ANNIE RACHELE LANZILLOTTO
L is for Lion: An Italian Bronx Butch Freedom Memoir
Yonkers, New York 2020

PREFACE

"Be careful on the street," my mother used to say. I'd also often hear things like "he's a kid from the street," describing someone with lost innocence. The street was a place where you could get robbed, raped or killed. It was the opposite of being in a safe place. No one looked out for you on the street, unless you forged alliances using your street sense and charm. The street was a place where tough guys and miscreants roamed, feeding on each other, chewing their way to survival.

Much of *The Hated Ones* takes place on the street. Out there in the free-for-all. Though, as we learn, inside places also promise danger. For street kids, anywhere can be a trap. A street kid carries the street in his head.

The Hated Ones is about street kids. Their ignorance, their vulnerability and their beauty. *The Hated Ones* uses the language of the street. The language is often filthy, violent and racist. But it is true to the time and place it describes. For all its darkness, *The Hated Ones* is a book about escape. Escape into the larger world from which one could peer, as if through a keyhole, into the little tiny microcosm that once was the street. A microcosm that once was the *only* world.

GETTING AN A

Tony Russo was slightly portly man; he had tight dark curly hair and a mustache. He was a very well-liked teacher. He was even a good teacher.

He liked the Italian tough guys in the class: John Squitelli, Sal Vitolo and me. Squitelli and Vitolo were born in Italy; they could speak in fluent Italian with him. I had only learned enough Sicilian from my grandparents to know the curse words. He joked with the three of us, calling us "disgraziato" and "pazzo," crazy.

We read Shakespeare in the beginning of the year. He made the stories come to life, impersonating the doting Polonius and the brooding Hamlet. Even Squitelli, who loved cars and machinery but hated Shakespeare, laughed at his Hamlet jokes.

"Why didn't Hamlet kill his father immediately?" Mr. Russo asked the class, holding the book open in the palm of his hand, suddenly very serious.

"Because he wanted to find the right time," said Sal.

"Sal's right," said Squitelli, "he could have killed him at prayer, but then his father would have gone to heaven." The way they talked it sounded like a gangster movie.

"Hamlet didn't kill him because he was a coward," I said. Everyone got quiet, like I'd said the wrong thing.

"Maybe he was a coward," said Russo. "Perhaps Hamlet had to struggle with his conscience to show us the difficulty of his choice." Then Russo walked up and down the aisles of the classroom quoting the "To be or not to be" speech verbatim.

One morning Russo called me to follow him to an adjoining classroom.

"What happened to you?" he asked, pointing to the bandage on my hand. The bandage was from an accident I'd had over the weekend.

I'd had a few similar incidents over the past two or three months. Black eye, nearly severed finger, and now this.

"Are you okay?" he asked, holding me by my wrist to see my palm.

"I'm okay," I said.

I had seen Squitelli smash a bottle at Party Palace a few weeks earlier. When he smashed it on the ground the neck of the bottle broke off perfectly as the body crumbled into bits. I was stoned when I saw it. After smoking pot and drinking beer at Party Palace with Joey D, I tried it myself, only with different results. For the few seconds it took to raise my hand, I was invincible. Like an interdimensional being, I could smash a bottle and walk away uninjured. I was made of glass; the bottle would become a part of me, dissolve into my being. But by the time the bottle hit the cement, it had ripped through my flesh. I was back on earth, sitting in Party Palace, a mere human, shards of glass dug into my skin. I laughed, saying I didn't feel anything. I didn't. Joey D called 911 and I went to the hospital to get stitches. My parents met me at the hospital. My father didn't look at me.

There was a lot going on at home. My father's gambling had reached even farther into our home. Now my older sister was loaning him money. Thugs had come to our house banging on the apartment door, demanding we open it, or else.

When Russo asked me what was wrong, my mind launched into a whirlwind. The bottle, my mother yelling at my father, my father sitting at the table staring into space, the bottle breaking into tiny bits into my hand, my father sitting at the table in darkness at night, the blood dripping down my fingers. For one split second, one stitch of time, the bottle was a spaceship and I flew through the darkness of space inside of it. I was the character in the science-fiction stories I had been reading. I was translucent, like a cosmic jellyfish. You could see the blue of space through my eyes. I was space itself, the light of the stars breezed through me. And then I was just flesh and blood again. I was just a kid in the park, breaking a bottle with blood pouring down my skin onto the ground.

"What's the matter?" asked Russo. "Why the puss?" I stared off into the distance, like I didn't see him, like I could walk through him.

"Nothing's the matter," I said.

"You're upset about something, right?"

"No," I insisted.

He reached out and rubbed my shoulder. "It's okay," he said. "You can tell me. Things are rough at home?"

I nodded yes.

"That's okay," he said reassuringly. "I can help you." He continued stroking my shoulder. I saw blood dripping from my hand, the thick redness of the blood inching across my palm to my wrist, then flowing down my arm. I saw the heavy red blood pulsing from my arm in big drops forming a soupy pool on the cement.

"That-a-boy," he said, rubbing my shoulder. Then he put his arm around me. "Come with me."

I followed him into the school bathroom. He lit a cigarette and handed it to me. "You're crying because no one understands the pain you feel, right?"

I took a drag on the cigarette and nodded in agreement.

He stroked my back again. As the tears trickled down my face, he reached out to touch my crotch. I jumped back. I didn't understand why he touched me down there. He did it again. This time I didn't stop it. I looked up at the crucifix hanging above the row of urinals, my body shaking as I continued crying.

"We can talk about these things," he said. "Do you want to talk about these things?" Still stroking my crotch, he said, "I can help you." I didn't want to be touched in my private parts. I didn't like it.

I threw the cigarette on the floor and stamped it out with my foot. Then I dashed out of the bathroom.

The next day, Russo called me out to the adjoining class, waving his index finger. I walked towards him.

"You know I want to help you, right?" he asked.

I looked at my feet and didn't say anything.

"Are you mad at me?"

I shook my head no.

Then he asked me if I wanted to smoke a cigarette with him.

I nodded yes.

He said to follow him to the bathroom. I did.

"They, I mean your parents, don't realize what all of this is doing to you at home," he said, handing me the cigarette.

I didn't say anything but held the cigarette with my thumb and index finger and took a long drag on it.

"I know they don't realize how the troubles are affecting you. Parents sometimes don't understand," he said.

Just talking about these things pried open the pain in my heart. I could feel the blood pumping in my veins, moving in my eye sockets, my skull. I could hear my blood moving in my head like a snake.

I took another puff on the cigarette, feeling tears crawl down my cheeks, like they had little feet. As I took a few fast drags, he reached down to stroke my pants. I felt disconnected from his actions. I didn't get an erection. I was both violated and comforted by the same gesture. He kept touching me as the tears rolled down my face. The tears felt like boiling blood, burning ducts into my skin.

Then he reached out, took my hand and placed it on his crotch. He humped into my left hand as I wiped the tears from my eyes with my right hand. He was doing to me the same things I was doing to Diana Perez, Rachel Fernandez and other girls I was messing around with in the neighborhood. The difference being that I wasn't getting excited.

"I know you don't try, but I can see how smart you are. You need to learn to apply yourself," he said, unzipping his pants, now putting my hand on his cock. "Yes, apply yourself," he said as he held my hand, bringing it towards his cock. "You're such a handsome and smart boy," he said.

My gaze meanwhile was fixed on the crucifix that hung in the bathroom. The whirlwind came again. I saw the bottle, the blood oozing thick and hot like wax. I saw my mother crying at the table. I saw the look of death in my father's face. I wanted to vomit.

Suddenly the bathroom door swung open. Russo stopped and backed away. A kid from another class walked in. The kid walked over to the urinal and peed. Then he washed his hands and left.

We'd sometimes spend thirty to forty minutes, maybe once a week, this way.

It became more normal as the semester continued. After a while, I stopped retching when he touched me. The other kids were jealous that I got called out of class. While they toiled on assignments, I was excused for being the teacher's pet. I was special.

Then he started unzipping my pants and playing with my private parts. But I was limp. I couldn't get a hard-on. I stopped seeing the blood dripping. I was somewhere else. I was in a capsule flying in the darkness of space. I flicked the switches, making the vessel change speeds. I traveled to the moon, to Mars. My capsule had even sailed to distant stars, like the stars I had fixed in my memory looking up in the night sky.

I even stopped crying. I became stoic. I stared up into the vacancy of the crucifix.

Would I go to hell if I died now?

He then gave up playing with my limp dick, pulled out his own dick and jerked off. Then he grabbed my hand, having me jerk him off. I looked away at the urinals. I focused in on the water in the bottom of the urinal, gurgling like a brook.

"You can get an A," he said.

"How so?" I asked knowing the answer.

"Put it in your mouth," he said, "and you'll get an A."

"I can't do that," I said.

He kept asking me to do this throughout the year. And I refused over and over. This all became so normal we even joked about my not sucking his dick.

On graduation day, we all said goodbye to each other. Our little lives were being let out into the bigger world. I was moving on to a private Catholic high school. Most everyone else was going to the local public school.

When I said my farewell to Russo, he held my face in his hand, saying "I'll miss you so much," as tears flowed out of his eyes. I cried too, now for the last time, my tears like scorching blood. I would miss him. I wasn't sure if he had cared about me, or what had happened. For those weeks, I'd felt the universe had cut me open and a knife had been plunged inside me. I couldn't believe the universe could be so cruel. But I couldn't have put it into those words. There weren't any words. There was an aching, like the feeling of a punch in your stomach after the punch has hit you. You can feel your heart beating, you feel the blood in your body pumping. Your heart races as your brain tries to find itself.

As I walked away from the school, I looked up at the giant golden cross. The Jesus on St. Patrick's church was nailed to a cross, but he was dressed in a robe. He was dignified, looking upwards towards heaven. He looked like a hero. I understood what the Jesus on that cross felt. He had suffered. He had come through something so terrible and wrong that he didn't want to think about it. But now he could look up at heaven. He could look up and feel that he had held himself together. He had had courage. He had never been a coward.

CLOSE TO THE EDGE

Holding a gun to my head, a kid with a black stocking over his face demands I hand over my cassette radio. The kid is flanked by another standing behind him, a stocking covering his head, too. My best friend Lan is only a few feet away.

I am fifteen; Lan is one year younger.

We're in the projects on one of the walking paths that border the rectangular grass area. The summer moon casts a silver light on the black tar of the pavement.

All I can hear is my father's voice in my head. *They're going to steal that radio if you keep taking it out.* And then images of beautifully illustrated rock album covers flash across my mind. Yes's *Close to the Edge*, Santana's *Abraxas*, the Allman Brothers' *Eat a Peach*.

"Give me the fucking radio!" the kid shouts louder this time. He is at least a foot taller than Lan or me, trapping us in his shadow. In the dark of night, our souls have fled from us, seeking sanctuary. Our bodies have aged and shriveled between heartbeats.

I stare back blankly, like there is only wind between my ears.

The kid with the gun is motionless, holding the muzzle to my head. The stocking on his face rises and falls with his breathing.

If I run, he'll shoot me in the back. If I swing my fist at him, he'll likely beat me to the quick and shoot me in the face.

I hear the plaintive screaming of angels in my head.

Instead of handing him the radio, I take off. Out of savage instinct, I bolt at full speed across the grass field. I wait for the bullet to come at me and punch me into another realm. I run as if I'll evaporate into mist, like a sheet of rain or a cloud in the sky.

But nothing happens. I glance back. To my inexpressible relief the kid isn't coming after me. I'm now a good fifty feet away.

"Dumb motherfucker," the kid yells, as he and his friend take off in the opposite direction.

Lan runs after me and soon catches up.

"That was fucked up," says Lan, out of breath.

Still running, I begin to slow down, my chest heaving.

We both stop running now. We're facing each other. Lan grabs me by the shoulders. We look at each other, our eyes wide and watery. This isn't an ordinary night.

"Are you all right?"

I nod affirmatively. In truth I'm shaking to the bottom of my fifteen-year-old soul.

"You sure?"

I say *yes* silently, incapable of speaking. I'm somewhere else, having an out-of-body experience.

For the rest of the night, Lan talks to me. It's a nervous kind of talking. He tells me about his favorite groups, the albums he loves most. He doesn't expect me to talk back. He's talking for both of us now, his words like an umbilical cord, nourishing me with oxygen and blood.

My bones still rattling, we smoke cigarettes on the park bench, not far from where the gun was held to my head.

Lan only stops talking at the end of the night when we finally say goodbye in the elevator.

I open the elevator door to the third-floor landing.

"You going to be okay?"

I nod yes.

"I'll call you first thing in the morning."

The elevator door closes. Lan continues to the sixth floor where he lives.

I swing the door to our apartment open then rush into my bedroom. I don't even say hello or goodnight to my parents. They have no idea what just happened.

The next afternoon, sitting in Lan's bedroom, passing a joint back and forth, he and I look out the window. Words have returned to me.

Lan's bedroom window has a view of the parking lot in the back of our project building. Being on the sixth floor, it's like we're on top of the earth. From Lan's window we can see the distant rooftops of other project buildings. At this moment, it seems as if our project complex is a chunk of Earth floating out in space, surrounded by a million years. The trees have a bright green shimmer as they sway in the gentle summer breeze.

We're listening to Yes's *Close to the Edge.* It's one of the many albums that are lined up on the shelf near the window where the record player sits. The title song blares out of the speakers. Lan's brothers listen to music at full volume, so this isn't unusual in his house. My father would have probably called the police if I played music this loud.

Close to the Edge opens with the sounds of birds twittering. The music conjures up a distant world: we're on another planet, sitting in a valley between mountains, there are spaceships flying overhead. In the sky on this planet there are two suns and a gigantic purple-red moon, even visible in the day.

Suddenly the band's music comes blasting out of the speakers, like a Titanic-sized UFO is crash-landing on our project building. The room shakes as the music comes screaming out of the walls.

"Yes is my favorite band," shouts Lan over the music.

"They're my favorite band with Bill Bruford as drummer," I say, leaning into his ear to be heard. It never occurs to us that we can lower the music.

"I know, I know. You like Bruford."

Lan likes the Yes configuration with Alan White on drums. I like Bill Bruford. Bruford is more of a jazz drummer, he plays offbeat rhythms—he's unpredictable. White is more of a straight-ahead rock drummer. Lan likes the live Yes albums, and I prefer the studio albums.

Lan and I have this discussion for hours while smoking weed. We talk about the worlds that Yes weaves with their music. Worlds of bucolic beauty. Mountain landscapes floating in space. Visions of a future in which humans have become spiritually and socially advanced. But Lan and I don't use words like bucolic. We don't know those words, though Lan writes reams of poetry that he sometimes shows me. But we're drawn to the poetic lyrics in Yes's songs. And we're fascinated by the interesting sounds of the instruments: mandolins, church organs, harpsichords, pedal-steel, nylon- and twelve-string guitars. There are also a lot of futuristic sounds in Yes's music: Moog synthesizers, Mellotrons and Hammond organs. The mix of ancient and futuristic makes Yes's music sound timeless. That, along with the legato singing and polyphonic harmonies, as if their vocals are sung by all the angels and saints in heaven.

Lan's mother bangs on the bedroom wall as she shouts over the music, asking us to lower the volume. She must have been banging for a few minutes. Lan turns down the knob on the stereo.

"Thank you," we then hear from the hallway. She doesn't sound angry; she practically sings her thank you. The music must have been at rock-concert levels.

"I can't believe what happened last night," says Lan in a hushed voice.

"I know, I totally freaked out."

"Why didn't you hand him your radio?"

This is not an easy question to answer. Sure, I was panicked, the black-metal gun to my head made me go blank. But there's much more to it than that. I had begged my dad for months to get me the radio. It's a Panasonic with a cassette player. Top of the line. We saved up for months to get it. Then he insisted that I shouldn't take it out so it wouldn't get stolen. So there's that.

But this little plastic box with knobs brings voices from another dimension. It tunes into frequencies on the electromagnetic spectrum that only initiated beings can hear. Or so we think.

"I mean, just running away like that from the kid with the gun, that was crazy," says Lan, lighting up the joint again.

Now the song's chorus rings out over the speakers.

I know Lan knows what I'm thinking. Despite the events of last night, the music calls to us. We're just kids, unable to explain that the music transports us to a safer place, a more beautiful place. A place less dangerous than the projects. Not as filthy. No dead steel factories or abandoned buildings in this world. In Yes's music we journey to places with mountains, rainbows and rivers.

"This might be my all-time favorite album," Lan finally says.

"Even with Bruford on drums?"

"Maybe," he draws out slowly. He's patting his head with his fingers. "I might put *Yessongs* on the same level with *Close to the Edge*."

I nod along with him, pleased.

"Do you think that guy would have shot me?" I say, suddenly changing the subject back.

"What?" Lan says. He always asks *what* when asked a question he's not sure about. There is nothing bitter or mean in Lan. He loves the crazy shit I do, but he wouldn't be the person to do a crazy thing. And he doesn't want to upset me.

"Do you think that guy would have shot me?"

"But he didn't shoot you."

"He put the gun up to my head."

"But he didn't pull the trigger." Lan smiles. "Maybe because he knew you were a sick motherfucker."

"But he was one click away."

"He was." Nodding now, he adds, "It would have been over in one second."

It's Lan's quick answer that gets to me. I think of how my body would have looked, splayed out on the concrete, a puddle of thick red blood pouring out from my head, like gas gushing from a busted fuel tank. I shiver for a second, but Lan doesn't notice.

"But you, you were a madman, running away like that. I mean, the guy could've shot you if you simply flinched." He waits a few beats. "You must have known that, right?"

I don't have an answer for him.

The joint between my index finger and thumb has gone out. I light it up again.

Wishing he hadn't asked his question from a moment before, Lan adds, "I'm just glad you're here and we can listen to music together. No one else hears music like we do."

I'm choked up by his words. We both know how close that call was. How close to death I had come. Close to the edge.

I take a pull on the joint and pass it back to him. We try to avoid looking at each other's watery eyes.

Then Lan reaches over to make the music louder as the final chorus plays on the stereo. The refrain on the title song of *Close to the Edge* reminds me of how I traversed the border of life and death, at one instant being both dead and alive. I hear the ghost echo of a gunshot in my brain. My blood feels cold and still in that moment.

Lan's mother bangs on the wall again, yelling, "Lower that damned music, I said!" taking me out of my trance. Her tone is exasperated, but playful. Then, for a split second, her voice sounds electronic and alien, as if it's been mixed through one of the Hammond organs in Yes's music. How did that happen?

Lan and I quickly glance at each other, doubling over in laughter.

We're both totally fucking stoned.

GARBAGE PARK

At 3:00 AM the garbage trucks pulled into the depot.

While the Ravenswood Project slept, great caravans of junk loudly rolled into the station. I woke up and—wondering how anyone could sleep—got out of bed and walked to the window. Pushing it open, I watched the trucks creeping back to the depot like defeated wolves returning from the hunt, hunched over, ragged. Great white heaps, they looked tired and dirty. Backing up into the garage spaces, they beeped loudly, huffing, making honking sounds.

"What's the matter?" my brother Virgil asked from his bed. He slept next to me, his bed perpendicular to mine, our heads nearly touching as we slept, as if the coils of our dreams were intertwined.

"Nothing," I said. "The noise is bothering me."

"Go to sleep," he said. "It'll stop."

As if he commanded it, the clatter suddenly ceased. From our third-floor window, I looked across from the Department of Sanitation to the adjoining park. We called it Garbage Park. There were basketball courts, handball courts and a full-sized cement baseball field behind the basketball court. In the darkness, the ground in the park looked clean and perfect. Far above the hallowed ground in Garbage Park loomed the Manhattan skyline.

I felt as if I was being lowered into the ground, plumbing the historical depths of Garbage Park.

There were stories that long ago, when Queens was farmland, Black people were tortured and buried alive in Garbage Park. Matty Jordan said that Moses Murphy, a slave who had escaped to the North, had been captured, beheaded and buried in the ground that is now Garbage Park, along with his wife and children. It was said that many slaves lay hidden in the earth beneath Garbage Park.

Evil lurked beneath the cement surface. As kids, we had no idea that our basketball dribbled atop a burial ground. That the echoes of our feet rumbled the ground below.

That night, as I looked above the empty park and gazed at the Manhattan skyline, the buildings were standing erect and blinking like spaceships. The Empire State Building proudly pointed to heaven, decorated in red, white and blue. From our view, the Chrysler Building stood sentry next to it.

There were no birds chirping, no signs of life. You might hear night birds in some other places on the earth, but not in Garbage Park. All the saints in heaven couldn't make them sing. The garbage trucks had chased them away. Papers twirled in the air, lifted by the trucks whooshing by. The street was dark blue, like a river of tar. Other than the movement created by the legion of trucks, the summer air was dead.

At any one time, two dozen garbage trucks were lined up on the sidewalk in front of the depot. Inside the garage another few dozen trucks slumbered. The entire neighborhood had become inured to the foul stench; the rotting odor of the garbage was no longer detectable.

It was in the handball court of Garbage Park, a few years later, that my brother Virgil said he could take Jethro Malone in a fight. Jethro and Virgil were both twelve, two years older than me.

Coming from one of many brothers, Jethro was stout and tough. Even though he lived only a few blocks away, in the Queensbridge Projects, he'd only recently started coming to our project block in Ravenswood. One day he was a new kid playing basketball with us in Garbage Park, and the next day he was the leader amongst us.

The day after Virgil had said he could take Jethro, Virgil and I had come home from St. Patrick's grammar school, books in hand. Jethro had stewed for twenty-four hours over Virgil's comment; he had the taste of blood in his mouth. We had no idea this had taken form; there was no warning. Jethro's dreams had mingled with the rotting garbage, the ghosts from his mind crawling out of his skull and slinking down 21st Street. In a heap of refuse, his pain began to shape into an anger, a fury that, by consuming everything in its path, only grew larger. The trash contained the decapitated skulls of slaves, the bodies of Blacks hung from trees, the ghosts of sins that lingered still in these Ravenswood Projects. The trail of death seeped into Jethro's brain at night and fed his fury, until it was too large to contain itself, and came tearing at us.

His rage was fueled by breathing in the dirty air. The stink worked its way up through our nostrils to our brains, invading our minds.

As we approached, Jethro stood in front of the lobby waiting for us. All our friends were there: the Vasquez brothers—Phil, Eric and Louie—Teddy Guzy, Simon the Zealot. But to my surprise, they were not there to stand with us, but to cheer Jethro on.

Across the street, a garbage truck blared and huffed, its lights blinking wildly, parking in front of a garage door, trying to warn us of the coming doom.

"So, you think you can take me?" Jethro shouted at Virgil. Before Virgil could say anything, Jethro punched Virgil in the face. Virgil staggered backwards and fell to the concrete floor, his palms flat on the rocky stone.

"And you!" he said, now coming towards me, "What do you think, you're a tough guy?" and slapped me with the back of his hand. I put my hand up to my face and felt the heat from the smack. I wasn't scared.

Hearing all the ruckus from the street my mother opened the window of our third-floor apartment.

"What the hell is going on down there?" she demanded to know. She'd frequently open the window to tell us to come up for dinner. Once, she opened the window and yelled at us not to cross in the middle of the street. Her voice boomed out of the window so loudly that a row of kids stopped in their tracks, walked to the corner, and crossed at the green light with us, like a colony of obedient ants.

"I said, what's going on," my mother repeated, no longer asking a question, her voice thunderous now, like the voice of a prophet coming from heaven.

Pointing at Jethro I said, "This fucking nigger just hit us." We didn't use that word at home and never outside to each other. It was a word Black people called each other. But I was so angry that Jethro had picked a fight with me and Virgil, I hoped saying this would slice through his heart and kill him on the spot. Perhaps right here, on this very spot, was a slave burial ground. As we stood atop the concrete, below its surface lay the remains of buried slaves, of abandoned children, some killed at birth, some dead from starvation. The bodies of women—raped, beaten—and the discarded bodies of men who crossed a white devil, lay twisted and tangled in the dirt below the surface, strangled by the earth, silenced. I didn't know what any of this really meant. All I knew was that I could marshal a legion of hateful angels by dropping that word. That word lay at the bottom of a great rubbish mound, accumulating power over the centuries. Just one word could tear the world apart.

It only made Jethro angrier.

"What did you say you little motherfucker?" he said, as he stepped towards me with his backhand across his chest, ready to hit me again.

Suddenly, walking towards the lobby entrance, we saw Charlie, my friend Vernon's older brother.

Looking at the worried eyes of the kids standing in a circle around us and the slap mark on my face, Charlie knew something had happened. As he looked up at my mother hanging out of the third-floor window, she pulled in the window and shut it.

"Why don't you boys go upstairs," said Charlie, pointing at me and my brother.

My brother and I walked into the project lobby, defeated. We took the elevator in silence.

That night, as we climbed into our beds to sleep, we talked around what had happened, not wanting to discuss it directly.

"You shouldn't curse," Virgil said. "And it was wrong of you to use that word. You could go to hell for that kind of language."

I became silent like I was listening to his sermon and taking it all in. Although I loved the crosses and red-eyed Jesus relics from Catholic school, the teachings about God and sin seemed unreal to me.

The sounds of the garbage trucks honking and beeping filled the room. Their red and green blinking lights flashed on the ceiling of our bedroom.

"Did you hear me?" he asked, noticing that I was staring into space as he spoke. "You shouldn't say curse words."

"I don't say no curse words," I said.

"Yes, you do—you say them to me." He paused for a moment. "You said them today."

"No, I don't," I said. "I don't say them."

He looked at me, knowing I was lying.

"Fuck you," I said. "I said it for you. I said it for us."

"Stop," he said. "It's wrong, you'll go to hell."

"I said it for us to make that asshole stop."

Virgil sighed and looked at me, disappointed.

Knowing I wasn't going to make my point, I gave up trying to be serious.

"Fuck you, fuck hell, fuck, fuck, pussy, pussy, fuck, fuck you, fuck, cunt, cunt, cunt, fuck."

Virgil turned over and put the pillow over his head so he couldn't hear me.

I smiled and turned over to go to sleep. It was the only victory I'd had that day. I fell asleep to the shadows cast by the trucks marching into the depot all night long.

* * *

Weeks after Jethro beat us up, Eric Vasquez found me in the project lobby. I had to fight my battles early to get them out of the way.

"Jethro says you're not allowed around here."

"What are you going to do about it?" I shot back. Eric's eyebrows arched in surprise. Eric pushed me and I pushed him back. Then I grabbed his shirt and pulled it up over his head and pummeled him with punches saying "Fuck you, you fucking scumbag." I wanted to punch his eyes out of his face. I had a few more skirmishes, being cornered in the project lobby, or threatened in Garbage Park. I addressed them directly.

We played a game Virgil made up coming home from school. The game was "who can walk the fastest." We played this game because the kids in the neighborhood were still taunting Virgil. If we walked quickly, he figured, people would have less of a chance to see us. As we took short quick steps, Virgil and I would look over our shoulders, left to right. We never talked about the game and why we played it; we just did it. Virgil's nervous energy washed over me and made me nervous too. If they were coming after him, they were coming after us.

"Where's your brother?" asked Ronnie Green, as we played basketball in Garbage Park one day. "He don't come out no more?"

Though Ronnie stood a foot taller than me, I shot him an angry look and didn't say anything. I wanted to kill him right then and there; my eyes were red on fire. If you talked about my brother, I hated you. I might have tortured my brother, but he was mine to torture, no one else's.

"But you ain't afraid of no one," he said, reaching his hand out for me to shake. "Yeah, you alright."

I shook his hand just to get rid of him, mumbling "asshole" under my breath.

A year later Virgil went to high school in Manhattan, on the Upper West Side. You couldn't see his school from our apartment window; it was nestled in the canyons and valleys of Manhattan buildings. The smell of the garbage couldn't reach that far across the East River. Virgil joined the wrestling team. He wasn't the scared skinny kid anymore. Lifting weights and training had made him muscular and confident. Going to high school in Manhattan, he was seen around even less. People would say, "I saw your brother walking from the train station; man, he looks different."

As Virgil got stronger from lifting weights, and with hormones raging through his body, he even put his foot down with me.

One time, playing basketball in Garbage Park, Virgil intentionally stuffed my shots, towering over me, making it impossible for me to score or even shoot.

After struggling for a few minutes, I threw the ball at him saying "fucking asshole." He took the ball and scored.

"You going to complain or play?" he asked. After a few more smackdowns, I waited for one more, then I took a swing at him, punching him square in the jaw as I had many times before. This time, he reached back and landed a punch right on my temple. My right hand automatically let go a counterpunch but went adrift as soon as the impact from his knuckles made my knees buckle.

* * *

Many years later I saw Jethro Malone playing handball in Garbage Park.

"How's your brother doing?" he asked. Having long ago made amends with Jethro I said, "He's good. You know, he's in school, playing sports." My brother hadn't been around the park in years. You see, Virgil had escaped Garbage Park. But many of us were still there, breathing in the dust from ancient bones. We had taken in the stink of death from our nostrils for so many years, our skulls were like cages littered with poisoned bats. The soot clogged our brains so badly that it even oozed out of our eye sockets. When we choked, we coughed up the bile of a thousand years of hatred.

"Do you think he could take me now?" asked Jethro.

"Yeah, Jethro, he could take you and me and the rest of us."

All I could think about was the silent bones buried in the dirt below the surface of Garbage Park.

THE CAT LADY

It was my idea to rob the Cat Lady, but I needed Lan and Joe's help, too.

"I've seen her stuff a wad of dollars in her pocket after buying a hundred tins of cat food at King Kullen," I told them. "She's rich."

"How could she be rich?" asked Lan. "She lives in the alley with her cats. She dresses in rags and smells like cat piss. She's fucking homeless."

"Look, I don't know how she gets money, but I know I've seen it." I paused and lit a cigarette. "I think we should rob her."

Lan winced at me like I was crazy. Joe kept his hands in his pockets then looked down at the ground. Joe knew that he was going to do anything we wanted him to do. We loved Joe, but he was our lackey, our guinea pig. Once, Lan hit Joe in the head with a baseball bat after I dared him to do it. They had to sew Joe's head back together. Then, when they put detectors in the library, I suspected that my book stealing days were over. I handed Joe a book on spaceship illustrations and told him to meet me outside. When the alert went off, it confirmed that they had installed those damned detectors.

"I don't know, Mike," said Lan. "This plan is a little cracked." Lan's smile showed both the caution and excitement he felt.

"Don't worry, I know how to make it all work." I paused, then continued, "She has a few hundred dollars in her pocket, maybe more."

I knew mentioning the money would stir their interest.

"A few hundred dollars, maybe more," I reaffirmed, not believing it myself.

"I'm not saying that we're going to kill her."

Lan looked at me like I'd just stepped on his foot.

"I don't even want to hurt her."

They both eased up, knowing I wasn't intent on killing the Cat Lady.

"We know the Cat Lady goes to King Kullen to buy cat food every Tuesday at about 2 PM, right?"

They both nodded their heads in agreement.

"But, wait a second," said Joe. "We've only seen her get cat food, right?"

"Yeah, so what?" I asked.

"That means she eats cat food, man."

"Joe, why is it that the first time you have a thought in your head it's about something stupid like that. And worse, you're interrupting my plan."

Joe looked sad. I was too hard on him.

"Where was I?" I snapped my fingers and said, "So we follow the Cat Lady into the alley after she buys her cat food. We must make sure that no one sees us. Then, when she's in the alleyway, I'll shock her by screaming at her. Joe, then you jump up and frighten her, putting your hands into the air. Lan, you then make believe you have a knife." I stopped and thought about it. "No, you use a real knife."

"What, I ain't using no knife," said Lan.

"Lan, I'm not saying that you're going to use it. You just hold it up, pointing it at her."

Lan still looked doubtful as I explained the next steps.

"As you guys distract and frighten her, I'll reach into the pocket and grab the wad of cash. That's where she stuffed the wad after she bought the cat food." I paused and looked at them. "Got it?"

"Yeah, got it," they both said.

It was a blazing hot New York City August day. The trees were still and bright green. They looked bent in the haze. The sun was so strong you could cook an egg on the sidewalk. We played basketball in the Department of Sanitation park across from the project building where we all lived.

When it was near 2 PM, we positioned ourselves outside King Kullen.

Just as planned, we saw the Cat Lady walking down the street. She was pushing her shopping cart. I saw bundles of clothes, linen and a plastic gallon of water in her shopping cart. The water looked dirty. She had ragged clothes on and a hood over her head, so only her twisted face poked out. She looked like a witch. She had bright blue eyes, chipped teeth, some missing, and made chewing motions all the time. I joked that Joe was right; she was always eating cat food.

"Okay, let's follow her," I said. The three of us kept pace with her about one hundred feet behind. When she stopped, we stopped. Did she notice?

As she got closer to the alleyway, I urged Lan and Joe to speed up. Now we were making quick steps to catch up. "Don't jog or be obvious," I whispered loudly. "You might scare her."

Now near the alleyway entrance, we were right behind her. She walked into the alleyway a few feet.

"Okay, now," I said. Lan and Joe rushed at the Cat Lady and I flung into action behind them.

I screamed "Ha!" stomping my feet loudly on the ground and raising my arms like I was going to attack her.

She turned around in surprise.

Then Joe made a sound like "argh" and flailed his arms about in order to frighten her. As Lan stumbled trying to flick open the pocketknife we'd gotten from the Five & Dime on Broadway, I reached out and put my hand in the large pocket on her dress. I felt around her pocket in the few seconds I had. I didn't feel anything. With no time left I pulled my hand out and started to run.

"Come on," I said, and we all ran.

We ran until we got to the other side of Broadway. No one had seen or followed us.

Out of breath, we all laughed, slapping each other's hands. "That was crazy," Lan huffed. "I can't believe we actually did it," Joe said. "Joe, that was hysterical. What the fuck was that you did to scare her? You looked like you were more scared than she was," I said, laughing. "You guys were funny." The truth is we had all scared the hell out of ourselves.

"So, where's the money?" asked Lan, still trying to catch his breath.

"You won't believe it," I said, now embarrassed. "I didn't get the money."

"After all of that, you didn't get the money?" asked Lan.

"I didn't. I fucked up." I didn't say that I got nervous and blanked out.

We were all a little relieved that we hadn't killed her, even by accident.

THE HATED ONES

John's cousins, Nooch and Antonio, emigrated to the U.S. from a small Neapolitan town when they were six or seven. When I met Nooch in Long Island City Park, he sat hunched over a bench, bending the thick steel wire in its interior. Antonio was short, but muscular and explosive. He had the air of violence in his flesh. He could launch guys two times his size into the air with one punch. When Antonio was pissed, he'd stomp his feet and bite his index finger, cursing and turning red. He wore a Hitler mustache and on his forearm was a tattoo of the Virgin Mary.

In the winter of that year, John and I started hanging out inside the old Scalamandré factory on 24th Street near Queens Plaza. During the Industrial Revolution, the old looms and the steady thwack of machines filled the factory with constant patter. Now, it was almost entirely silent. We found an open door that led to a dead-end stairwell, but you couldn't get any further into the building beyond that. It looked like a room people were taken to be raped or murdered. At one time, Scalamandré's walls held hundreds of workers, making silk that was exported to the world. Now, empty and abandoned, Scalamandré was an oasis for vagrants, a temporary shelter to sleep in on bitter winter nights until a cop decided it was time for them to get up and move on. For us, it was a perfect place to hang out, smoke pot and drink in the dead of winter.

At the Scalamandré factory, John confessed his loyalty and respect to me, passing joints back and forth, drinking from a forty-ounce Olde English bottle. Sometimes while crying. This was in stark contrast to the John I'd seen punch a dog in the face for barking at him. At the Scalamandré factory, I got a glimpse into his human soul. In the prison chamber of the factory, John pled guilty to kindness and charity, as if they were sins in the real world. And then he might tear into a rage.

"Anyone ever fucks with you, I'll kill them," he said. The light hanging on the wall buzzed against the stark silence. I took a slug of my forty-ounce.

"You know why I do this for you?" he asked, punching the wall with his right hand.

I shook my head saying no. I truly had no idea.

"It's because you're good to your mother and father," said John, tears running down his face. "I respect that. I respect someone who knows how to treat their mother and father."

John had been to my house and met my parents. I don't know what he did or said, but he must have done or said something to my parents that showed this respect. Despite John's wild hair, black leather jacket and coarse demeanor, my father liked him.

"Yes, Mr. Conforto," and "Hello, Mrs. Conforto." My father asked about John; he appreciated that John had the sense to be polite in our house.

When we left Scalamandré later that night, high on pot and drinking beer, we stopped at Vacarro's Pizza, under the elevated train station.

"You got money?" John asked.

"I got three bucks," I said and bought pizza for both of us.

Then afterwards, John pulled out his own money and bought a drink. He didn't share it with me. I stared at my pizza feeling lonely and stupid.

But John could make up for it, in his way.

When John found out that Chris Crumb was calling my girlfriend Ginny a slut and teasing her in public, he was pissed.

"We should fuck Crumb up," he said.

"Yeah," I said. I wanted to fuck up Crumb. Shaved head like a punk and over six feet, Crumb was a bully, but he always acted like he was my friend when I saw him.

One night, I met John at Long Island City Park.

"I saw your boy Crumb today," he said.

"Fuck that asshole," I said. I wasn't planning to do anything. I was happy to let things drag along as they were. As long as Ginny continued to suck my dick in the project hallway, I didn't care who said what.

"Well, I told him you said hello," said John.

"Why'd you do that?"

"I told him you said hello with a punch in the face," said John.

"You hit him?"

"Yeah, I said 'Conforto says hello,' and then I japped him, knocking him on his stupid ass."

My mouth hung open, eyes blinking.

"I did it for you asshole. The least you could do is say thank you."

"I appreciate it, man," I said. "It's just that I never had no one kick someone's ass for me."

A few weeks later, at Scalamandré, John confessed again that he'd kill anyone for me. I was puzzled but honored. It's good to know people who'd kill for you.

Then, months later John joined a gang called the Hated Ones. To be a member you had to be resigned to your death. Death could come in any way. Getting stabbed in the face, shot, or pummeled by a brick to the head. I knew all the members. Jimmy "Gestapo" Schumacher who expressed his undying faith to Hitler, wearing a Nazi helmet and long Nazi trench coat. Chris "Ness" was average height and had narrow eyes, like he was always squinting. Though Ness had hands like bricks, he was the best graffiti artist of the Hated Ones. Standing at five feet, Mikey Ferrone was built like a midget Hercules, his chest muscles bulging and articulated. Ferrone lifted parked cars off the ground just to slam them back down and see what broke. Then, there was Junior, the sole Puerto Rican of the group. Junior had a thin face, like he was underfed. He had scars on his cheeks that didn't look like shaving mishaps. His neck was long and knobby, like a chicken's. His bald head sat way above his shoulders, like it didn't belong to his body.

John designed the logos for the Hated One's dungaree jackets. He even recruited his father, a tailor, to stitch the Hated Ones patch on each of the jackets. John didn't pressure me about joining the Hated Ones. "I know you ain't into gangs and shit; you're too busy playing guitar and getting pussy." I did very little talking as a kid. I never explained things. I nodded or just didn't say anything. The less I said the more people seemed to understand me. While I wasn't a member of the Hated Ones, I hung out on the street corner by the liquor store smoking pot with them.

That winter, we were in the park, standing around with our hands in our pockets, taking them out only to smoke. The air was cold and wet like a snow was coming. The sky was streaked chalky white.

Then suddenly, there was a group of Puerto Ricans surrounding us, calling us out to fight them. As they milled about, I wondered how all of this was arranged.

"What's this about?" I asked John.

"These spics asked out my ex-girlfriend Gina," said John. "And one of them went out with Schumacher's girlfriend."

But the girls decided to go out with them, I thought to myself.

I said, "That's fucked up."

"Who you going to take?" John asked me.

I thought I wasn't in the gang, I mused silently. But I said, "I'll take him," I pointed to one of the short Puerto Rican kids I thought I could take.

The kid saw me pointing at him. Then we walked towards each other, staring each other down from a few feet away.

Despite the cold, Ness took his shirt off, baring his muscular chest and Christ tattoo. Schumacher wrapped a red bandana on his forehead. Ferrone took his gold cross off and put it in his pocket. Where was Junior? John folded up his Hated Ones dungaree jacket and asked Teresa Fasano, standing on the sidelines, to hold it.

John ran towards the Puerto Ricans with his fists clenched to fight.

I now stood face to face with my Puerto Rican.

"What the fuck is this all about?" I asked him. I didn't yet hit him.

"It's you stupid white dudes, man. I ain't got nothing to do with this," he said. "I didn't fuck no white bitches."

Everyone else was already fighting.

I put my hands up and shadow boxed toward him; he shadow boxed toward me.

"I don't want to fight you, man. I'm not even in the gang," I said.

"You ain't in the gang?" he asked, now thrusting his fists at me, circling close around me. I looked at the other fights. Schumacher had his guy on the ground in a head lock. John fought a big guy with a goatee, striking him repeatedly across the face with a pair of brass knuckles. Ferrone had smashed a garbage can on one guy's head and now stood over him triumphantly.

"We don't have to do this," I said.

"Look man, like I said, I had nothing to do with this shit either," he said, then took a swing at me. I ducked and took a swing at him, hitting him square on the nose. As he staggered backwards, I kicked him in the balls. From the corner of my eye, I saw John now looking at me.

Then before I knew it, the fight came to an end. The leader of the Puerto Ricans whistled, and they all ran off.

Afterwards, we all sat in Party Palace, the high throne in Long Island City Park, and bragged about the ass we kicked in the shivering cold. The girls, Teresa Fasano and Mary O'Malley, had reunited with us to celebrate our victory. Even if they weren't the cause, they were the reason the fight went down, but none of that mattered now. John described how he fucked his guy up and Schumacher demonstrated how he wrestled his guy to the floor. Even Junior showed up.

"They wasn't real Puerto Ricans," said Junior, defending his people. "They was more like niggas than Ricans. Ricans wouldn't fuck nobody's girlfriends."

Everyone nodded.

"And Conforto here," said John. He stopped talking and pointed at me. I was nervous he was going to say that I didn't even try to fight my guy. I wasn't sure how much of the fight he'd seen. "Conforto kicked that little spic's ass," he said, slapping my hand. "Did you see that Jimmy?" he asked. Jimmy said, "yeah he's one of us now, that motherfucker. He bad ass," then passed the joint to me. The joint warmed my hands.

I took the joint from Jimmy, as I held Mary O'Malley's hand, and looked at the dark sky way above Party Palace. The dark of the night looked like it went on forever.

THE RING

Walking into my mother and father's bedroom, I go straight to her chest of drawers. She keeps her jewelry in a little compartment next to her undergarments. The ring is there, just like I expected it to be. I pick up the ring and look at it. It's made of white gold and studded with diamonds. Up until then I had just been stealing little things: necklaces, earrings, and things that didn't get noticed. A little bit at a time. Then I'd go down to the husband-and-wife jewelers on Steinway Street and sell them for what I could get. They'd weigh the gold and give me money, maybe twenty or thirty dollars. Knowing it was stolen, and that I was a dumb kid, they gave me less than market value.

I hear the apartment door opening, so I grab the ring and shove it into my pants pocket. Taking big steps, I rush out to the living room, out of breath.

My father drops his keys on the table, looking at me suspiciously. "Home from school already?" he asks.

"Yeah, we got out early," I say.

"Are you doing laps in the house?" he asks.

"Push-ups," I say quickly, catching my breath.

"Oh, okay. Do you want to go for a slice of pizza?" he asks.

"No." I'm brimming with guilt right now; I don't want to be around my father. The ring is burning a hole in my pocket. I'm imagining the guitar I could buy with this ring. It's got to be worth many hundreds of dollars. I could buy a white Fender Stratocaster like the one Jimi Hendrix plays. I'll probably have enough left over to play video games at the smoke shop. For a few weeks, I'm going to live it up.

And I'll get away with it. Right now, my mother is furious at my father. Night after night, she yells at him at the dining room table.

"How can you just sit there?" she asks.

He doesn't say anything.

She takes another sip of red wine. Her words begin to slur.

"Get another job. You-have-to-do-something," she shouts each word one at a time, as if not speaking in sentences.

He doesn't look up. He keeps looking down at the crossword puzzle on the table, smoking his cigarette, tapping ashes in the ashtray. Unlike my mother, my father doesn't drink. Gambling has destroyed him enough. He remains sober, all too aware of the pain he's caused his wife, his children.

"We don't have anything. You keep lying, you keep gambling and we don't have anything. We can't pay the rent this month. We-can't-pay-the-rent."

My mother's not going to think I stole her ring; she's going to think my father did. He's the one who needs the money.

I leave the apartment and go up to the 6th floor where my best friend Lan lives.

"I got the ring," I say.

"You took the ring?" he asks, wincing. We'd talked about it, but he can't believe that I would do something so bold, so evil. Lan is like a brother to me. Being half Puerto Rican and half Black, he's slightly darker than I am.

"Yes," I say, smiling but worried. This was my mother's favorite ring.

"What are you going to do?" he asks.

"I'm going to sell it at the jewelry store," I say. "Let's go now. I can't keep this thing in my pocket."

We walk to the jewelry store on Steinway Street. He can't get over how gutsy this move is.

We get to the store. The owner is reading a newspaper.

"What do you have today?" he asks. He puts the newspaper down and reaches for his magnifying glass.

I hand him the ring.

He looks at the ring and then looks at me. He applies a liquid to the ring to determine the amount of gold.

He calls his wife over.

I can tell he's trying to hide his excitement. His wife looks closely at the ring, then looks at me. I can see she's excited too. This is an antique ring, with delicate designs and settings. The diamonds are subtle, but they shimmer.

"How much do you want?" he asks.

"How much do you think it's worth?" I ask.

"I don't know, maybe three hundred," he says, waving his hand, like he's not that interested.

"Three hundred and fifty?"

He looks at his wife; she bites her lip, nodding in agreement.

"So three hundred and fifty?" he says.

"Yes," I say, my voice trailing away, now realizing I could have gotten more. But three hundred and fifty should be enough to buy a guitar.

His wife goes to the register to get the money and hands it to her husband.

He counts out six fifties, two twenties, and one ten in my hand.

"Three-hundred and fifty."

I look down at the money.

"So, okay?" the man says.

I'm hesitant to walk away from the deal.

"Okay?" he repeats. He can't believe his luck.

I fold the money up and put it in my pocket. The man then hands the ring to his wife. It's a gift from him to her and for a great price.

* * *

"I can't find my ring," my mother says, storming out of the room. She looks at my father.

"What?"

"Have you seen my ring?"

"Me?" he says.

"Yes, you. I'm talking to you," she shouts at my dad. I knew it would go this way.

"Did you see the ring?" she now points at me and asks.

"Uh, no," I say, shocked.

My mother is rabid. She tries to light a cigarette but can't because her nerves are shaken. She throws the matches across the table.

"Maybe it was the maintenance man," my father says. He lights a cigarette too.

My brother Virgil and my sisters, Connie and Jenny, are now in the living room. It's a witch hunt. My father is the one with blood on his hands. My hands are alabaster white.

"If you did this," my mother says to my father, now crying, "I'll never talk to you again, you fucking bastard. You know how much that ring meant to me."

"I would never do that to you," he says, nervously smoking. He can't help but be guilty. He's always guilty. He's the one who lies, borrows and steals. He's the one who could steal the ring, who would steal the ring to get more money to gamble or to pay off an urgent debt. Except he would have gotten eight hundred to a thousand for the ring. With that thousand dollars he could have placed a few bets at the horse track, he could have been a sport for a few days, taking us out to a Chinese restaurant, buying comics for me and my brother. That's what he loved most about money. He loved to spend money on other people, show them that he could.

But not me. I'm greedy. I think about how smart I am. I've outsmarted them all. Only twelve years old and I've tricked them all. While I ran away with the golden egg, my father is nailed to the cross. He deserves to be the one nailed to the cross. He's the one who fucked up, not me.

As my mother rants, I'm thinking about the guitar I'm going to buy. It's going to be beautiful, just like the guitar Hendrix played at Woodstock. Beaming in brilliant white, with a whammy bar. When I play it, I'll sound just like Hendrix, roaring, on fire, thrusting my body back and forth, as I bend the strings, the notes shooting out like flaming bullets.

BIG BEN

Lan and I saw Big Benny in the project lobby almost every day. He was always drunk, or drinking. You could smell the liquor reeking from him and sometimes see the fifth of Wild Turkey hanging out his back pocket.

At about six foot two, with a big belly and small potato head, Benny loomed over us like a mountain. He had a slightly gray short Afro. His eyes, sunken into his already faraway head, were covered with a thick film, making it look like he couldn't see. We said he had snot eyes.

One morning we saw Benny in the lobby, smoking a cigarette.

"Hey Benny," I said, in a mock drunken voice, as I swung the project lobby door open, almost hitting Benny in the face. I knew he hated me. He hated Lan because Lan hung out with me.

"What, you think you is the Mafia, boy?" he asked me, slurring his words, leaning to one side, as if ready to fall at any moment now.

"Yeah, I'm in the Mafia," I said, "and so is my father. He kills assholes for a living. He'll kill you."

Benny mumbled something about me being a stupid fucking dago. Though he stood almost a foot above me, I wasn't afraid of him.

"Fuck you, Benny," I said.

"What boy?" he asked. Benny's hands were slathered with grease. I'd seen him rubbing a stick of butter on them, putting it between his fingers. He did this to treat his hands after burning them with cigarettes and lighters. He'd fall asleep with a burning cigarette between his fingers, not even waking up as the embers singed his skin.

I didn't answer him, so Benny shouted back at me.

"I said what boy?"

"You heard what I said, you drunken hobo," I bellowed at Benny.

Lan and I ran to the elevator door, laughing hysterically.

Before he could take a step towards us, we shut the elevator door and started pressing buttons.

As the elevator door closed, we heard Benny muttering "dumbass motherfucking dago."

The next day, Lan and I came back from playing stickball in the park. It was a hot August day. The sun was raining down on the concrete, pouring into the concrete cracks like lava. Since no one had air conditioners, the air was dead and still, even in the project apartment building. The stairs were lifeless, the gray painted walls looked worn and monotonous, like the hot summers had beaten them down too. Every so often you'd swallow a sudden puff of urine smell from the stale project air.

As usual, we saw Benny standing in the lobby. His hands were slick and shiny with butter.

"Hey b-b-b-Benny," I said, taunting him.

"What you said, boy?" asked Benny. He staggered, hardly able to walk. When he spoke the alcohol smell streamed in waves towards us. I liked the way it smelled. It smelled like danger.

"I said, b-b-but-but, Benny."

"You is one dumbass dago motherfucker," said Benny.

"You dumb and you drunk," I said.

Suddenly Benny stepped towards me. Instead of taking a step away, I reached out to push him and shoved him backwards.

He looked down at my hand surprised that I shoved him, tripping back with the force.

Even I was stunned by how much he lunged back. He kept stepping backwards until his head hit the window of the lobby. Since the lobby windows had shelves about every two feet, Benny's head hit three shelves, one at a time, as he slid down the lobby window—thump, thump, thump—all the way to the floor. When his head hit the floor, his chin sank into his chest and his feet shot out like bullets from their sockets.

Lan and I looked at each other.

"Oh shit," said Lan. "He's dead. You've killed him."

I had to have been white as a ghost. I gulped and said "I didn't push him that hard. I didn't mean to kill him."

"I know but he's dead now."

Then, like a whale firing out a blast from its blowhole, Benny exhaled a gust of air out of his lungs. His lips fluttered. He started breathing again like he was pulled back from death.

"Oh shit," I said to Lan. "Let's get the fuck out of here."

THY KINGDOM COME

Father Francis hired me to work in the church rectory—the office attached to the priest's residence. My job was to fulfill requests from parishioners for baptism, confirmation, marriage and various other records.

This was my first day of work—ever.

When I arrived at the rectory, I was greeted by Father Francis wearing white shorts and a T-shirt.

We were alone in the rectory office.

"You decided to come after all." Wearing sneakers and holding a bag with tennis rackets, he gave me a quick rundown of my responsibilities, explained that for the next few days I'd just answer the phone, take inquiries and collect numbers and that later he'd show me how to answer inquiries.

Then the phone rang. I stared at it, not knowing what to do. As he leaned over me to answer the phone, I smelled his cologne.

He talked for a few minutes, then hung up.

"Next time, you pick up the phone," he said smiling.

"I have to leave now," he said, grabbing his rackets.

"Where are you going?" He looked like he was going on a date. The two of us having spent time together, he allowed me to joke with him, like we were friends.

"I have an appointment."

"Is she good looking?"

"You have no idea what I have to do for the church."

"Do you get around to playing tennis?"

"Sometimes," he said, winking. He looked up as an older woman emerged from the rectory house. "This is Lucy," he said. "Lucy will bring you lunch when you're working; she's the housekeeper." Lucy smiled, then walked away. Being Sicilian, she spoke little English.

We talked for a while longer, then Father Francis left the rectory office. I was by myself now.

Sitting in the rectory office with a few hours stretched out in front of me, I thought of what I could do to while away the time.

Using the Rolodex of baptismal and confirmation dates and names sitting on the metal file cabinet, I made a few random prank calls.

"Is this Mrs. Ryan?"

"Yes, it is," an older lady's voice answered.

Staring at the cross that hung on the rectory wall, I said, "This is God calling you."

"Oh my, this is God? Well now, I better sit down," she said.

Having information about her date of birth and home address gave me authority. How did I know her baptism date? What else did I know? Whoever I was I was sent by God or the devil. I might have been the only person she spoke to that day.

After talking for a while, I said, "It's been nice speaking to you, Mrs. Ryan."

"God, please say hello to my husband." This stunned me. "Tell him I think about him every day." She was crying.

I was silent for a few beats. "Mrs. Ryan," I said, after collecting myself, "Mr. Ryan is in the best of places. He wishes you well. He's smiling on you."

Her voice grew a little quiet now.

"Well, I appreciate the call."

"Bye, now. God bless you," I said.

Then I hung up the phone.

I made a few more prank calls to pass the time. Most people hung up once they realized it was just a stupid kid on the phone.

Then Lucy appeared in the office with a bowl in her hand, holding it with a towel.

I could smell the garlic and other aromas coming from the bowl.

Lucy was short with a wide round face and bright eyes. She looked like my grandmother. I took the bowl from her. She walked back into the rectory house.

After a few days, I realized that I'd sometimes have long periods of idle time. I brought weed with me so I could step outside and smoke when Father Francis was out and the coast was clear.

A month in, working four hours two days a week, I was settled in the routine. Father Francis had showed me how to look up records, create the certificates and mail them. I was comfortable enough to start smoking pot outside the rectory after I arrived.

Stoned, sitting at my desk, surrounded by crucifixions, pictures of Christ, I could get back to making prank calls.

Then the phone rang. I picked it up.

"St. Rita's rectory," I said.

"Yes hello," a voice answered. It was a boy's voice, about my age.

"How can I help you?"

"You want to help me?" said the voice, whispering like we were being overheard.

"Yes, how can I help you?"

"I need help with lots of different things," he said. "Are you a priest?"

"Yes, I'm a priest," I said.

"I wanted to know if you could help me jerk off, Father."

"Help you jerk off? That's disgusting."

"I know I'm disgusting," he said. "I'm going to hell, Father. I want you to tell me that I'm going to get fucked in the ass by the devil in hell, Father."

Not sure what to say, I said, "you filthy fucking asshole."

"Oh yes, that's right Father, I'm a dirty filthy fuck."

"Wait, are you jerking off now?" I asked. I didn't occur to me that I could just hang up.

"Yes, jerking off to you, Father."

"No that's not what I meant." But before I could finish my sentence, he released a long and loud exhale.

"Thank you, thank you, our Father who art in heaven." His voice trailed off, then he hung up. The phone went dead, the fast-busy sound repeating like an ambulance siren.

Needing to take a break, I wandered into the church. I kneeled in one of the pews, staring up at the stained glass. I asked God to forgive me for allowing that boy to jerk off on the phone. I said four

Hail Marys and two Our Fathers.

Then I went back to the rectory office.

I looked up at a picture of Christ on the wall. I saw the sadness in his eyes. I felt like Christ at that moment. I realized that Christ was a guy who got fucked over by other people. He took their shit. He was the dupe of a mean world.

I finished out the day, answering the occasional call. I even read the science-fiction magazine I had brought.

When I left the rectory with the money I had earned, I bought twenty dollars' worth of skunk weed.

The next day at the rectory, I called Tracey, a girl I was messing around with, to meet me at the rectory. I knew I'd be alone. Lucy came out only at lunch. Otherwise, she was somewhere in the catacombs of the rectory.

"Meet you where?" she asked.

"At the St. Rita's rectory, where I work," I said.

"You work there?"

"Yeah, but no one's ever here," I said. "We could hang out," which meant make out and grope each other.

When she arrived, I moved fast, taking her out to smoke a joint just outside the rectory doors. I told her to go back into the rectory office; I'd be there in a minute.

I dashed into the church and kneeled in one of the pews. I asked God if he could deliver Tracey to me all the way. She was so pretty, had such beautiful lips. I couldn't stop thinking about her. I crossed myself and got back up.

Then I met her back in the office, closing the door. I leaned her up against the office table, pressing my body on hers, kissing her. I put her hand on my crotch motioning for her to rub it while I ran my hands up and down her body, kissing her wildly.

She stopped.

"Hold on a second, I hear something," she said.

I stopped and waited. I told her it was nothing.

"Don't you think this is a little weird, making out in the rectory with crosses everywhere?"

It didn't occur to me that it could be weird.

"Don't worry about it, close your eyes."

She did, but I could feel that she wasn't there anymore. The spell had been broken.

"Listen," she said, looking at her watch, "I have to go. I have homework to do."

I said that I understood. But as she was leaving, I thought about who else I could call.

After all, I was working.

FAT ANDY

That could have been me almost killed as I sat on the schoolyard steps getting high with Ferrone. But it wasn't my turn, yet.

Only a few weeks earlier I'd bought a ten-dollar bag of weed on credit from Fat Andy. Fat Andy was a new dealer in Astoria Park. A little taller than I was, he had a tiny bald head that sat on his pear-shaped body like it didn't belong there. Despite his menacing look, he smiled a lot. Andy was about twenty, maybe five years older than me.

That day Ferrone bought a bag of weed.

"What about you?" asked Andy.

Shoving my hand in my pockets I said, "I ain't got no money."

Andy looked at me and said, "I'll give you a bag, but you gotta pay me when you have it." I nodded and took the weed.

Days later, I was with Ferrone and we saw Andy. I had ten dollars on me. I thought of reaching into my pocket to give Andy the money, but I didn't. I just nodded at him. He didn't ask me for it either.

Over the next few weeks I'd see Andy on the street, but I tried to avoid him. I either pretended I didn't see him or walked across the street so he wouldn't see me.

Then, at the St. Demetrius fair, under the elevated train station, I ran into him. It was a July night, hot and sticky. Ferrone and I had walked back and forth through the fair, seeing friends and talking to girls. Being stoned made the fair magical. There were multicolored lights dangling from the streetlamps. There were small rides bedecked in blinking neon. The occasional train passing overhead was like thunder roaring from heaven. As I laughed with Ferrone, I saw a sign that read "Magical Tea-Cup" in perfect neon green. It was so fiery I swear I could hear the snapping and buzzing of that neon. I kept my eyes fixed on the sign. Then I got a tap on my shoulder. I turned around. It was Fat Andy.

"Hey, you think I don't see you avoiding me."

"I ain't avoiding you," I said, leaning in now. The summer night and the lights swirled around me. I was somewhere else.

"Where's my ten dollars?" asked Andy. I didn't respond.

"Don't be a fucking smart-ass," he said now.

"I ain't being a smart-ass," I said, leaning even more towards him, a smirk on my face.

I looked around and saw that Ferrone had walked away. Suddenly all of the lights faded away; it grew dark like a rain was coming.

Now Andy was flanked by two long-haired tough guys. I looked behind me; there was only a wall there.

"I'm going to let you go this time," said Andy. I nodded like it was nothing. Then Andy wound his arm back and smacked me with a backhand. I stumbled. The two thugs stepped in. As I staggered backwards, Andy launched a direct punch to my face. I fell to the ground. All around me was silent and pitch black. If I got up, I knew I would be crushed.

"Now, get the fuck out of here you little punk. Don't ever fuck with me again," said Andy.

Suddenly Ferrone reappeared.

"Hey what happened?" he asked. We both knew he'd abandoned me.

Then, weeks later, as I sat in the schoolyard with Ferrone, we saw a guy, maybe eighteen years old, limping as he walked down the street. He looked hurt.

Ferrone passed me a joint. I took a toke and looked on. Then we saw a group of thugs running after the limping man. It was Andy and his two henchmen. When they caught up to him, one of the longhairs spun him around and put his arm behind his back, holding him up so Andy could punch him. Andy threw a few hard punches in the face and in the stomach. The guy fell to the ground.

Then I saw Andy pick something up. Now I unbent my knees to stand up a little. I wasn't stoned anymore. Ferrone passed me the joint; I waved it away. Andy had picked up a brick and lifted it over his head. He brought the brick down on the guy's face. I heard the sound echo in the schoolyard. It was like the crack of a baseball bat. Ferrone and I looked at each other.

Andy and his henchmen ran away. Surprisingly, the guy got up. His face was bloody. He looked stunned, like he didn't know where he was. "Pay your debts next time motherfucker," I heard Andy say though I could no longer see him.

Neither Ferrone nor I called 911. That was something other people did. We watched the guy stumble away, blood on his shirt, his face smashed and swollen.

I lit a cigarette. My hands were cold and shaking.

THE WINGED MAN

Joey Grace walks down 34th Avenue heading towards the army barracks, a Panasonic cassette radio dangling from his hand. It's nighttime, the winter air is cool and soft. The moon's light follows Joey as he saunters down the street, as if guiding him.

Despite the quiet frosty night, Joey blasts Led Zeppelin from his boombox. The sound is so loud it's like a calliope ringing out to an approaching town, announcing the pending arrival of a traveling circus. Jimmy Page's thundering guitar screeches like a high-speed train, metal on metal, as Plant's voice repeats call and response to the guitar sounds. It's as if Joey is a traveling sound machine, ploughing through the silence of the night, bending trees, warping the cement street.

I wave hello to Joey, pointing to my ear.

"Hey man," says Joey, reaching out his hand. Joey is tall and lanky. He has soft wavy blonde hair. As we shake hands, Joey's face breaks out into a big smile.

"I can't hear you," I say, pointing now to the radio.

Joey turns the radio volume off. It's as if the night is swallowed by the radio dial. The din of crashing music echoes in my mind, banging around my skull like a loosened demon.

"I'm heading to the barracks," says Joey. His eyes are watery and red. "Wanna go smoke a joint and have a few beers?" He shows me the six-pack of Budweiser he has in his other hand.

I nod yes and now we're both heading towards the barracks.

Someday it would be called Kaufman Astoria Studios but now it is a broken-down and abandoned army barracks. We go to the barracks to get high, make out with girlfriends and take refuge from the cold. Inside the barracks, it is dark. I can hardly see what is around me. I could be stepping on a rat's nest, or a dead body for all I know.

We never sit down in the barracks. We stand around, our hands in our pockets, warm air issuing from our mouths turns into mist. We go there because the cold is cut a little bit by the barracks walls. It is dank and musty inside. You can only see shades of things, like pieces of broken walls, pipes hanging from the ceilings. There is a dripping sound somewhere in the interior.

Now inside the barracks, Joey puts the six-pack and radio down on the ground.

He lights up a joint and takes a long drag on it.

He puts the music back on, but not so blaring this time, so we can talk. The music would echo throughout the steel chambers of the barracks, ricocheting off the walls, multiplying like a million hammers.

Joey's playing Led Zeppelin's *Physical Graffiti* album on cassette.

Now handing the joint to me, Joey shakes his head to "Custard Pie" and starts to play air guitar. We all love Led Zeppelin, but Joey is beyond devoted. He wears a dungaree jacket with a beautiful painting of the Led Zeppelin swan-song design. The image is of a man with wings flying in the sky, arching back, his hands reaching up and behind him. I don't realize it now, but one day I'll see that the image reminds me of a crucified Christ. Whereas Christ is nailed to the cross, the winged man in this image is in a free-fall. As the name suggests, he is in a swan-song position, perhaps falling out of the sky to his death. But the winged man looks powerful and alive. He might be dying but he's rejoicing in his death. He's dying beautifully.

"No one like Zeppelin," says Joey.

I shake my head in agreement. Of course, I love Led Zeppelin too. But Led Zeppelin is Joey's life.

Joey pulls up his dungaree sleeve to show me a tattoo of the swan song on his forearm he's recently had done. He would cover his entire body in Led Zeppelin designs if he could.

I laugh at the tattoo.

"You're fucking crazy man," I say.

"You're crazy too, motherfucker," says Joey.

I can tell that Joey is very high already. He's probably had a six-pack or two. Despite his love of intoxication, Joey is gentle. In fact, he's mostly an incredibly kind and generous person.

"You're crazy, man," repeats Joey. "That's why I fucking love you, man." Now he's reaching out to shake my hand. Joey stares at me as if from the depths of his soul. He's still smiling, but now I can see tears forming in his eyes.

"You're a brother to me," adds Joey now.

"You're a brother to me, too," I say.

The truth is, I really like Joey. I'm not afraid of him, like I am of some people in my neighborhood who will stare at you while they declare their undying love for you. In our neighborhood, some people's protestations of love are a little frightening. As if they would announce their devotion and love just before they stab you to death with a rusty nail.

But not Joey. Everyone loves Joey and Joey loves everyone.

"I'm going to the train tracks later," says Joey.

"I have to go home. I can't go."

Joey likes to go down to the train tracks. He likes to lie down sometimes between the rails, let the trains roar over his head. I won't do that with Joey.

"It going to be fun. It's a little cold tonight, but I have my beers and weed." Joey has only a T-shirt and dungaree jacket even though it's about thirty degrees above zero.

"You sure you want to go tonight?"

"Yeah, I'm sure," says Joey. The truth is Joey is fucked up every day and pretty much all the time. It's not like this is a bad time or a good time. He goes to the tracks to get a thrill. It's how people like us spend our time. We do a lot of dumb shit, wasting time, wasting our lives, sometimes putting our lives in peril just for kicks. I have friends who hang from rooftops to write graffiti. When you see the work they've left behind, you can't imagine the contortions and how they risked their lives to leave a mark on a wall.

As we finish the joint, Joey tells me about how much he misses his father. His father, a cop on the Brooklyn beat, is dead, having been shot in the face in the line of duty only a few years ago. His father is a hero, a decorated officer. But a picture in the newspaper doesn't cover the hole his father's loss has made in Joey's heart.

"I wish I could have him back," says Joey. His eyes are steely, but they are flush with tears. Joey's crying is silent but heavy.

"I know, man. I'm so sorry, bro."

"I know. Everyone is sorry. I'm sorry. You're sorry." Now Joey is slurring. It's incredibly hard to see Joey suffer like this. Especially Joey. There is something angelic and perfect about him. He bears the weight of the world's suffering on his shoulders. Not just his father. In his tears, he carries every homeless person frozen to death on the street, abandoned children left on a concrete stoop in a baby carriage crying out for help.

Now, grabbing his radio, Joey points to the beer.

"I'm going to get some more; you can have these." We've already had two beers each.

"You're leaving already?" I ask.

"Yeah, I want to get down to the trains."

As we part ways on 34th Avenue, I shake Joey's hand, then lean in to give him an embrace. His face is now completely wet with tears. Some of the tears have frozen on his face.

"Listen, be careful tonight, okay?"

"I'm always careful," says Joey.

As he walks away, Joey raises the music volume. I laugh a little. He doesn't give a shit that he's making a ton of noise and must seem like a maniac to anyone who passes by.

A few days later, I run into my friend Tommy on the street.

"Did you hear about Joey?"

"No, what happened?"

"Joey went to the tracks Wednesday night."

"Yeah, I know, I was with him before he left. He goes all of the time."

"I heard he walked into an oncoming train. He must have been incredibly drunk."

I can't believe what Tommy's just said. My heart drops. I see Joey's gentle smile in my mind. I hear his soft voice. It just can't be. Not Joey.

Then I think, sick as it sounds, maybe the victory is Joey's despite what everyone says. Unlike the rest of us who will drag through our failures and disappointments, Joey got out through the escape window.

I imagine Joey wearing his swan-song jacket, his wings extended and unfurled, arching his body as he dives into the wind, being blown away into forever.

THE ANGEL IN THE STAIRWELL

We arrived at the theater early; it was nearly empty. Lan and I slunk into the red velvet seats. I rolled a joint, licked the rolling paper then twisted both ends.

As we toked on the joint, passing it back and forth, a girl we knew, Diane, walked in and sat next to us; she was trailed by a shorter dark girl. I looked straight past Diane and at the other girl. Even in the dimly lit theater, with pot smoke curling around our faces, I could see the silhouette of her pretty face.

Sitting next to me, she said her name was Rachel Fernandez. Rachel had perfect straight black hair, dark brown eyes and light-toned brown skin.

"Do you like Neil Young?" I asked her.

"I don't know who that is," she said. She didn't have an accent, like many of the Puerto Rican girls in my neighborhood did.

"You're about to see a Neil Young movie," I said, passing her the joint. She waved her hand, saying no.

"Diane wanted to come so I came with her," she said. I stared at her lips as she spoke. They were full and moist. I knew she'd be great to kiss. I was happy that Lan and Diane were sitting together, away from us so I could talk to Rachel. The only thing I didn't like about her was her name. Rachel was an old lady's name, but this Rachel made slow moves like a cat.

We talked a little about music. She said she liked disco. I liked rock. I said that I was a guitar player.

"You look like a guitar player," she said.

"What does that mean?" I asked.

"You have long hair and you're cute."

I touched her arm as we talked; she didn't seem to mind.

"I like to dance," she said.

"Can you show me how you dance?"

"Here, now?" she asked.

I nodded.

She wiggled in her seat.

I didn't tell her that I'd been practicing for a dance contest with another girl. I told her that my sisters liked disco. I knew every Donna Summer song on the radio, every note, every word. But I didn't tell her that.

I imagined kissing her as she spoke.

"Are you listening to me?" she asked. I nodded my head up and down. I vaguely heard her discussing the new discotheque that had opened on Steinway Street. As she continued speaking, I lost track of what she said, as if I was mesmerized by a snake charmer.

"Do you mind me saying that you have beautiful lips?" I said suddenly aloud. It was like I'd thrown a rock through a window in a silent house. It was like someone else said it, not me.

She ran her tongue across her lips now and looked at mine.

"O dio mio," she said.

"Did I say something wrong?" I asked. "Are you okay?" I thought maybe I'd gone too far.

"I'm very good. Very good."

"I feel good too," I said. "I like you."

"Really? You mean that?" she asked, now holding my hand, squeezing it.

I leaned in toward her face. Our lips touched. The heat from her breath gently landed on my lips.

Then we started to kiss. At first, they were soft, delicate kisses. Then we collapsed into each other.

Lan and Diane looked over at us, laughing. Now Rachel and I kissed, tightly holding hands, sometimes gently rubbing each other's thighs.

I didn't watch any of the film. For an hour we tongue kissed and embraced like our lives depended on it. By the time we left the theater we were girlfriend and boyfriend.

When I met her after school, all of the older boys were impressed that she was my girlfriend. She wasn't only pretty; she was shapely and knew how to move her hips when she walked.

"How'd you get Rachel Fernandez to go out with you?" the older boys asked. I shrugged my shoulders. I didn't have to know why. I was able to make girls like me. If I liked a girl, there was a good chance she'd like me back.

Rachel and I made out everywhere we went. After school we'd go to the stairwell in my project building to kiss and grope each other. My favorite spot was just above the sixth floor. The building was six stories, but there was another set of stairs that led to the roof. Even though the roof door was usually open, I liked to take girls to the nook between the sixth floor and the roof. It was my private room.

One time on the stairwell, I was rubbing my pelvis up against her backside, kissing her neck, like I did with Diana Perez. I was trying to unbutton her pants and pull them down. Rachel's backside was taut and round, not an inch of fat on it. The skin on her rump was brown and smooth, like the perfect skin on her face. She'd been letting me pull her pants down more and more and hump her from behind. This time, I pulled her pants down all the way exposing her ass and placed my cock in between her ass checks.

"What are you doing?" she asked.

"Don't worry, it's okay," I said.

"I don't want you to get me pregnant," she said.

"I won't," I said, completely heedless of what that meant. I kept thrusting my cock between her legs, rubbing along her pussy and the crack of her ass. I pushed and pushed. From her moistness I was able to push faster and faster until I came. But I never entered her. I'd only been circling around her pussy, rubbing my cock near the general hot area of her parts. Between that and the perfumed smell of her kisses, I was beyond blissful.

We went back to the rooftop on many occasions, our love cemented by the mingling of our youthful sex aromas.

One day my friend John Squitelli told me that I shouldn't be going out with Rachel.

"She's no good for you."

Surprised but curious, I wanted to know why.

"You're too good for her, man," he said. "She's holding you down. The guy you were was a free spirit," said John, emphasizing his words by spitting on the ground. I kept thinking about Rachel's perfect ass and how she moaned when I humped her. "You gotta learn how to let things go," said John.

I listened to his speech. It didn't make any sense to me, but I decided I would take his advice. I didn't want no girls slowing me down. I could always get a new girlfriend, or just another girl. All I had to do is want a girl and I'd get her. If I saw a pretty girl on the bus, I could meet her. If I saw a pretty girl in the park I'd get her.

So the next day when I met with Rachel, after I humped her ass on the roof, I told her we had to break up.

"Why, why, why are you breaking up with me?" she asked, crying. "I can't have you leave me. I love you," she said, tears pouring down her sweet beautiful face. She was so cute when she cried. But I didn't care. I couldn't tell John I didn't have the balls to break up with her. I wasn't afraid of John, but there was an honor I couldn't describe that I had to maintain.

"We have to do this," I said, now enjoying the fact that she was crying.

"No, no, I love you. I love you."

I stroked her arm, comforting her. Someday none of this will matter I told her. As the light in the hallway flickered on her face, my eyes did laps up and down her cheeks, loving their roundness and softness. Her luscious lips puckered, tears making them even moister. I held her hand and gently kissed her.

"I thought you loved me," she said.

"I do love you but I have to do this," I said, like the wise old fourteen year old I was. I had to let her go for both of us, I explained, wiping the tears from her eyes with my thumb.

Weeks later, John said that it was good I broke up with Rachel. "Why?"

"She's been fooling around with me now," he said. "She's too much of a slut." I felt duped but wouldn't show it. I was both hurt by his dishonesty and by what I perceived as her infidelity. "Yeah, she's a slut," I said, the image of her angel face in my mind, the flowery smell of her body enveloping me entirely.

Nothing but a slut.

THE KING'S KLATCH

I'll admit that I wasn't a heavy metal fan. But our friend, Joe, insisted that we had to see King Diamond. This was 1980.

"This is great music, man," he said. "They're amazing musicians. It's not just guitar shredding."

"What's the band's name again?" asked Lan.

"King Diamond," said Joe with a straight face.

Lan and I laughed.

"Trust me," pleaded Joe, shaking his head to underscore the seriousness of the band and his opinion of them.

But Lan and I were doubtful. Our love of heavy metal music stopped at Black Sabbath and Deep Purple. But Joe was deep into groups like Megadeth, Iron Maiden and Motorhead. He had the albums, wore their T-shirts. Lan and I were more into progressive and psychedelic rock, groups like Yes, Jethro Tull and King Crimson. Psychedelic groups wrote songs about other worlds, about the love of the universe, of knowledge. That kind of crap. They transported us out of the drab Long Island City world that we grew up in, factory and project buildings, and placed us into new fantastic realms. The album covers were fairytale-like. A chunk of earth floating out into space. Extraterrestrial creatures. And the instruments they played. And played well. Mandolins, acoustic guitars. Moog synthesizers. Spacey far out shit. Somewhere between *Lord of the Rings* and *Star Trek*. This is where we wanted to be. Lost in the cosmic swirl. Not stuck in the dismal shithole of the projects, or in the satanic hellhole of heavy metal.

But Joe persisted. He begged. Let's face it, he didn't want to go alone—all the way to L'Amour in Bay Ridge, Brooklyn, from Queens. And he wanted us to like his music, too.

We had to take the train to 62nd Street in Brooklyn. To make the long train ride bearable, Lan and I smoked a joint in between the train cars. We held onto the train handles, passing a joint with our free hand, swaying with the stopping and starting of the train. The great thing about riding between train cars was that you could do anything. You could smoke cigarettes, pee on the tracks, or vomit into the rushing air if you had to. This was the NYC subway system. There were no rules.

Before we went back into the train car, Lan and I popped a hit of mescaline. Joe never took drugs. He just watched us as we slowly devolved into idiots.

Sitting in the train car, we laughed and joked. The train moved slowly, creaking its way to Brooklyn. There was garbage swirling around the train cars and graffiti on the train walls. As littered and filthy as the train car looked, it began to glow and shimmer.

By the time we got to our stop, the mescaline and weed had fully kicked in. Walking down the street you could hear the buzzing of the neon signs, like they were speaking to you in some secret electronic language, luring you into the stores upon which they hung. Maybe there were aliens hiding behind the counters in the stores.

From the outside, L'Amour looked like a humdrum bar, but when the door swung open, the bright velvet curtains and ornate chandeliers gave the impression that you'd stepped into a medieval dungeon. The mescaline was now fully pumping through my brain. The colors were sharper, and the sounds were more articulated. I could hear wind in the drum cymbals and radar signals in the guitar notes.

There were at least three floors inside the club and little alcoves with couches where you could make out or smoke weed in a more private place. Since the band hadn't yet started, we roamed around the club exploring its hidden chambers.

The castle-like atmosphere was enhanced by the chalky white-faced zombie fans who sashayed through the venue. The dead look in their eyes was a little ominous. Along with the now thundering guitar sounds and heavy bass riffs pounding the walls, it felt like we were secretly being led into a slaughter. Machines blew out curls of smoke that twirled and twisted in the arena lights, taking on the changing colors. There were lights flashing and blinking to the music. The only thing that was missing was lightning and rain.

Style-wise, Joe, Lan and I were completely out of place here. We wore simple dungaree pants and T-shirts. We didn't have gothic outfits, make-up or long purple fingernails. And our hair was more Afro-like than long.

Suddenly all attention turned toward center stage. It became completely dark and suddenly very silent. The zombies gathered around us; I wondered if they would try to eat us in a savage frenzy.

Then the lights flooded the stage. The band, as if materializing out of nowhere, began playing. The music sounded like the groan of a gigantic metallic whale chained to a cage in Hell.

As the thick smoke from the stage cleared, a bejeweled coffin emerged from the blackness. I could hear grunting from the zombies around me. Were they alive, or were they dead already? Mouths open, hands now extended, they eagerly waited for the moment their leader would tear into them, like a devil released from Hell, ripping open their stomachs with his fangs and claws.

Joe kept pointing to the stage. He was whispering to me and Lan, but we couldn't hear him.

We wanted to laugh but between the mescaline and the weed, we were scared out of our wits. I swear I could see bats flying around us. This was getting serious now.

And then, the coffin slowly opened. The leader of the dead zombies, King Diamond, stepped out of the coffin. He stuck his tongue out and made threatening faces, opening his mouth wide, pushing his eyeballs out of his head.

As soon as he started singing, the zombies began shaking their long hair in unison with thudding rhythms, as if their hair was clapping to the music. Shaking their skulls likely also made their brains turn into a mushy pulp.

We just stood in awe, our hands by our sides.

Singing into a microphone shaped like a human skull, King Diamond's face was painted with blood, as if his zombie worshippers had chewed into his cheeks. At some point, King Diamond's body seemed to spin and whirl to the music. The stage was now a vortex where demonic wizards and spirits swam in an embryonic cell. Their bodies liquefied and oozed in the placental walls, their essences melting to the hypnotic rhythms and screaming guitar frequencies. This was way beyond just music. This was a consecrated transfiguration. Like we were witnessing the beating heart of the universe, everything that had ever lived and died. All existences metamorphosing into a single blood cell that pulsed and pumped. It was nothing short of a possession.

On the train ride home, we were followed by goblins and demons. Some of them were disguised as ordinary passengers. We kept moving to different cars to escape them and because we couldn't stop laughing. And every time we stopped laughing, we got serious, concerned that some evil spirit would attack us with spikes and toss our severed limbs to other flesh-eating fiends. We weren't sure if the train was going down into Hell or just west and north back to Queens.

Somehow, we made it home, stumbling back to the Ravenswood project building we lived in. It was almost four in the morning. A pink sliver streaked the sky, suggesting that the world would be once again wrested from the demons.

SHAMING SHOES

When Gina LoRusso convinced me that we could win the King of Queens Dance contest, I pretended to give a shit about dancing so I could get into her pants. For as long as I could remember, my sisters had tortured me with disco songs like "Come to Me" and "Love to Love You Baby." I'd grown up hearing Donna Summer, Gloria Gaynor and the Bee Gees streaming from their bedroom.

I sat behind Gina in seventh grade at St. Patrick's Elementary School. Sometimes I quietly hummed disco melodies in her ear, tapping my foot to the beat. I made her laugh, almost getting her in trouble a few times. I would do anything to make out with Gina. At twelve, I had made out with every girl I could, many in the back hallways, or the stairways, some on the street, or in the park. I'd only flirted with Gina so far.

Sometimes I walked her home from school. She never gave me a kiss goodbye.

One time, as I gave her a hug and said goodbye just outside of the apartment complex where she lived, I met her older sister Donna.

"So, I hear you like disco," Donna said, leaning on the silver wire fence that lined the pathway to her building. Of course, I didn't object. I nodded in agreement. When I heard disco songs, I'd daydream about making out with Gina and running my hands all over her body.

Donna kept speaking but I didn't pay attention. Drifting out of my fantasy I heard her say that Gina and I would be cute in a dance contest. Then she said that the dance school on Crescent Street was having a contest in a few months. She was an instructor at the school.

"You two are adorable together. You'll win on looks alone," she said, combing her hair with her fingers. Her hair was long, thick and black like a shawl. "I can teach you, for sure." It occurred to me that she didn't mind having a conversation with someone who wasn't speaking to her. She wore pink tights that fit her perfectly.

The next week, I walked to Gina's house on the way home after school on Tuesday to talk about the dance contest. When I arrived, her father and mother greeted me in the parlor, looking me over. Her father's eyes were big and saggy like he was tired of life. There was death in his eyes. He never said a word to me. Her mother asked me questions about school. What subjects did I like? Did I get good grades? She had black hair in a bun; shiny earrings hung down from her ears. The earrings were oversized and ugly.

Then Donna came out of her bedroom. She had on a tight red dress that made her backside look like a perfect tomato. Her shoes were shiny and had sparkles on them.

Pointing to my sneakers Donna said, "You'll have to get dancing shoes. The judges won't like those." I looked down at my sneakers. They looked foreign to me, as if worn by a homeless man. I couldn't pick up my head to look at her after she said that.

That weekend, I bought a pair of Capezios at a shoe store on Steinway Street. They were bone white and pointy at the tip. The sole and the heel of the shoes were light brown. I would never let my friend Tony Gallo see me in these shoes.

The next time I went to Gina's house, I said I had a surprise.

"For me?" asked Gina, looking at Donna.

"Kind of," I said, now realizing that I seemed cheap for not buying Gina a present.

"Well, open it."

When she saw that they were Capezios for me, her face dropped. But Donna's repeating "you got them, oh my god, oh my god, you got them," made Gina smile finally. Donna took them from my hands, looking them over, running her finger along the heels, like they were precious objects. She silently told me to put them on, pointing her index finger at me. I sat down on a chair in the parlor and put them on. I tried to distract Gina and Donna by directing them to a painting on the wall when I noticed I had a hole in my sock. Then I slipped the Capezios on quickly.

I stood up, looking down my legs at the shoes on my feet. I hated them.

"Those shoes look cute," Donna said. Gina nodded her head agreeing. Their fussing over the shoes annoyed me.

"Now, let's get to practice," said Donna.

Donna counted our steps as we moved back and forth. "Put your hands on her waist," she said. "Like this?" I asked like an altar-boy, making sure not to touch the wrong places, the places I wanted to touch. If my hands slipped down Gina pushed them up.

One time, during practice, Donna left the apartment to go to the store. Her parents weren't home, either. Gina and I were dancing close, our cheeks touched. She turned her face quickly and her lips brushed across mine. "Oh sorry," she said. I was hurt that she felt it was a mistake.

"Do you think I can give you a kiss?" I asked. Gina looked long and cautiously at me with her dark eyes. Her skin was smooth and brown. She was pretty. I argued with Tony Gallo saying that she was the prettiest girl in school. He disagreed. He thought Mary Malone was the best-looking girl in school.

"Maybe you can kiss me after we win the contest," she said. "Now let's practice." I put my hands on her little waist just above the curve of her hips. As we danced, I looked at the confirmation photo of her that sat on the mantle above the old fireplace. In the photo, she clasped her hands tightly in prayer. Her perfectly round dark cheeks beamed from the white embroidered dress she wore. Her lips looked smooth and soft in the picture. I wondered how her lips would feel on mine.

"Just one kiss?" I asked.

She looked at the apartment door, took a quick look around just to make sure no one was there then said, "Okay, give me a kiss now." She blinked, her eyes pools of bright brown in the light.

I leaned in to give her a kiss and opened my mouth. She had closed her eyes and only offered her closed mouth. I had been kissing girls in the back stairway, full open-mouth kisses, so I was surprised by her move. I wound up landing a slobbering wet kiss on her lips. She opened her eyes.

"What was that?" she asked wiping the wetness from her face.

"I don't know, I thought that maybe we would, you know, do a real kiss," I said in a mopey voice. Didn't she know how to kiss like that?

"Well, I don't do that with boys, at least boys I'm not going steady with."

To my mind dancing was going steady.

"Let's continue practicing before my sister comes back," she said, heaving a breath of air from her mouth, placing her hands on my shoulders. "Well?" she asked, waiting for me to put my hands on her. I was still stunned from rejection. Then I moved into position, my hands slid on her waist. Her hands alighted on my shoulders like delicate birds. She began counting and our feet began moving again. Looking down at the Capezios, I detested them with all my guts. Stupid ugly shoes, dumbest piece-of-shit shoes I've ever seen. I wore them strictly to dance practice and then put them back in the box when we were finished and carried them home in a bag. I didn't want to scuff them up on the streets is what I told Gina. And dancing was stupid, too. And I really hated the songs, though I knew them all word for word by now.

The following Tuesday, I came over. No one but Gina was home.

"Where's Donna?" I asked.

"At the dancing school," said Gina.

She held out her hands, motioning for me to come in closer to dance. I put my hands on her waist, then let them move down to just above her backside. She didn't flinch.

"Now, let's go, one, two, three, one, two, three," she said, staring down at our feet. I moved my feet according to her instruction. As she looked down, I looked at her face, her lips.

"One, two, three."

I let my hand drift down even further, now grabbing her bottom.

She reached down to move my hand up.

"You're not moving your feet right," said Gina. She was right, I was just getting aroused. I didn't even know I had feet at that moment. I had hoped she would see the erection pressing against my pants.

"Could we try again?" she said.

"Can I have a kiss first?"

"If it will make you concentrate better," she said, like she didn't care whether we kissed or not.

"Yes, it will."

"Okay, you can kiss me but not like last time," she said.

"I won't kiss you like last time," I said, defeated but willing to take whatever I could get.

Her lips were moist and pink. As I looked at her pretty face, she closed her eyes. Then eyes still closed, she pursed her lips, then gently licked them.

"Well, are you going to kiss me?"

"Can you open your eyes while we kiss?"

"I don't want to open my eyes."

"It's not the same if you close your eyes."

"This was your idea," she said.

"Can I put my hands here," I said, placing my hands on the curve of her backside.

"Not really, but do it already. My parents will be home any minute."

Before she could close her eyes, I leaned in to kiss her, feeling the heat from her lips, both of my hands on her perfect round little rump. She closed her eyes, then opened them again, full and bright. I squeezed her rear harder now and rubbed into her pelvis. She started leaning into me, positioning her leg between mine. My erection was as hard as a doorknob at this point.

For a few seconds the heavens had opened.

"Okay, okay," she said, wiping the moisture off her face, pushing me away. "Now, isn't that enough?" She was flushed.

"Not really," I said, my hands now in my pockets apologetically.

"Let's get back to dancing," she said.

"Okay,' I said, sadly looking down at my Capezios, like this was all their fault.

I didn't go to Gina's next week. Two weeks later I showed up, but had to leave early, I said.

"You have to put the time into this," said Gina. I wanted to leave early so I could meet Dolores afterwards. She did everything in the stairway with me. I didn't tell Gina that I was meeting Dolores.

In the weeks that followed, the talk of the contest ceased. I went once or twice more, always meeting with Dolores afterwards. By the time I got to Dolores's apartment, we'd hardly say hello after I knocked on her door. She'd see the heat rising from my reddened skin, take my hand and make out furiously with me in the stairway until I came in my pants.

Then I just stopped going to Gina's after I realized there was not going to be any more kissing involved. I went straight to Dolores's thinking of Gina all the time.

The last time I came home from Gina's house, I stuffed the Capezios in the white box they came in and put them up in my bedroom closet.

GUIDO IN THE AISLES

Tommy Vitolo wore white slacks and polished Capezios and adjusted the pinky ring on his finger out of habit. He called me "caveman" when I showed up at school in dungarees, my hair in a puffed Afro.

"You ain't bad looking," he said. "But you gotta do something to tame that pubic hair on your head."

I reached up to feel the tight short curls on my head.

"You'd make a good Guido. You might even get laid," he said, laughing.

But I did get laid. Even though I didn't dress in white pants and fancy shirts, I kissed girls in the hallways. They pulled their panties down for me. I kissed girls I hardly knew, girls I met in the street or in the park.

But all the girls liked Tommy. He was handsome, with thick full lips and radiantly blue eyes. The darkness of his hair made the brightness of his eyes shimmer, like sapphire stones on fire.

Tommy lived by Rainey Park, the rows of houses surrounded by projects, directly across from the Citibank building in midtown Manhattan. Tommy sounded like his father when he ranted about how college was for faggots and hippies. He made it a point of bragging that he did better in all the honors classes we were in together. On the bus home from school he made fun of me for reading Freud's *Civilization and its Discontents*.

"I don't got to read no book to get good grades," he said.

Then, playing with his thick gold cross, moving it up and down the thick rope chain it hung from, he said, "Only phony liberals read." He pronounced "liberals" slowly, emphasizing each syllable, as if it were a three-word curse.

"I'm a liberal because I read?" I asked. I didn't even know what liberal meant. I thought it meant someone who believed in free sex, or who dressed in hippie outfits. I came from people who hated politics. My parents were blue-collar Democrats who didn't vote. They didn't believe in unions. Everyone was out to get them. They didn't trust government, corporations, or the cops. Liberals feared people like my parents. They liked them only in textbooks.

"No, you read because you're a freak," he said.

I laughed at the word freak.

"I'm going to Papa Gallos Saturday night, if you want to go," said Tommy, suddenly changing the subject.

Papa Gallos was a discotheque on Steinway Street. My ex-girlfriend Diana talked about Papa Gallos. She'd go dancing there with her sister, Maria. This made me jealous. All I could think about was Diana being groped and lusted after by Guidos and Puerto Ricans as she spun around under the blinking discotheque ball. She said she only went for the dancing and I believed her. But the more I thought about her wearing those tight-fitting pants with the gold sparkly belt on her waist, the more desirous I became. Just hearing the name Papa Gallos gave me a hard-on, making me want to run to a private place and jerk off, thinking about Diana shaking her ass at those boys, knowing she'd be turned on by the attention, even if she rejected it. I could be one of those lecherous Guidos, wearing cologne and a gold cross, grabbing my crotch when the girls walked by.

"Okay, I'll go," I said.

"Do yourself a favor," said Tommy, looking me up and down, winking. "Lose the rock concert get-up." He smiled. "Not for nothing, but I don't want you to make me look bad."

"Fuck you, asshole," I said, "I got plenty of shit to wear." But I didn't really. All I really had were those wretched Capezios that didn't go with my dungarees or any of my shirts. I wouldn't tell Tommy about the Capezios. They were either terribly out of fashion or exposed me as a closet Guido. And Tommy was curious about me because I wasn't a Guido. I wasn't like his other friends. I was filled with exotic facts, which sounded funny when we were both stoned. For instance, I knew that it would take nineteen thousand years for a modern spaceship to get to Alpha Centauri, the nearest star. Tommy cracked up when I said this as I passed a joint to him back and forth in the project hallway.

The night I went to Papa Gallos I wore white baker's pants that came tight at the ankle. I also wore a red nylon shirt that made me look like a box of chocolates. Even my sisters laughed at me.

"I can't believe you're going out in that getup," my sister Tina said.

"It looks good," I said, staring in the mirror, brushing my hair.

"You look like a Guido."

"I thought that was a good thing," I said.

"Guidos are idiots," she said.

Tommy laughed when he saw me.

"Look at you, you look like you stepped out of an '82 Cadu." Cadu was what Guidos called Cadillacs.

"Come on, man, I look good," I said, not so sure of myself.

"You're alright. Don't worry about it."

I arrived at Papa Gallos. Blue smoke pushed up from the dance floor. Girls in flashy tight outfits danced to the music, hot and lusty. I smoked a cigarette, looking at everyone. There were pretty girls, some with too much make-up, others wearing tight pants or tighter skirts. And I looked like the other guys, clownish, with silly mustaches and gold hanging from their necks. Tommy and I had a beer by the bar.

Two girls walked up to Tommy.

Tommy gave them both a hug. He knew everybody.

"This is my friend," he said, pointing to me. I smiled at them both, but longer at the smaller one. She was shapely, very pretty. When I said hello to her, she smiled back. They talked briefly to me, then raced to the dance floor when a song they liked came on.

"Who's the smaller one?" I asked Tommy.

"Miriam's mine, bro."

"How do you know she's yours?"

"She likes me, can't you tell? You can have Martha."

I didn't say anything. I knew from her smile that Miriam liked me. They waved to us both from the dance floor to join them.

I danced with them, not committing to one or the other. I looked at Miriam in the smoky darkness. Her lip gloss flashed in the brilliant lights. Her lips looked wet, waiting.

We all danced, Tommy pairing off with Miriam. But she moved away. Then Martha sashayed towards Tommy, motioning at him to dance with her. They started to dance together.

That left Miriam and me alone.

Miriam reached for my hand. I took it, dancing apart, but smiling and mimicking her moves. The music pumping, the lights flashing, we both laughed. I talked a little, leaning into her ear. Mostly we looked into each other's eyes, as if there was something I'd find peering into their depths. Her eyes glowed like hot cinders. A fast song came on, we danced wildly, throwing our arms out, spinning.

"Let's take a break," I said, out of breath. "You want a drink?"

"Sex on the Beach," she said, which made me chuckle.

When I came back with the drinks, she was applying red lipstick, pursing her blood-dipped lips.

I handed her the drink.

"Here's your Sex on the Beach."

"What'd you get?" she asked.

"Hopefully sex later tonight," I mumbled so she wouldn't hear me, or maybe almost hear me.

She made a face knowing I said something smartass.

"Just beer, I mean," I said.

She asked how I met Tommy. I told her that we were both in honors classes at school.

"You're smart too, like Tommy?"

I didn't say anything.

"Where do you go to school?" I asked.

She said that she went to Bryant High School, as she put the glass up to her mouth, leaving the outline of her lips on the glass. I loved the way lipstick smelled. It smelled of women, of sex.

We talked for a while longer. She recited Shakespeare's "marriage of true minds" sonnet, which impressed me. Then I performed the "to be or not to be" scene verbatim. When I finished, she clapped with both hands, still holding her cocktail.

As if now volleying back and forth, she then recited "Shall I compare thee to a summer's day."

As she spoke, I drank in her fragrance, the sound of her voice; I drowned in the rhythm of the poem. I was washed out to sea by the way her hair fell on her shoulders, losing all sense of myself. I was a thing destined to kiss her, fondle her, and run my hands all over her body.

Suddenly, she put her hand up. She had to listen to the song now blasting out from the speakers.

"My favorite song," she said, pulling me by the hand, running to the dance floor and pumping her hands up to the beat. As she mouthed the words to the song, I followed her steps, moving along with her, grinning, giggling.

She spun around and shook her hips at me. I pulled her in close, my lips touching her neck. When she turned around, her eyes had softened, they looked at me, up from my legs to my face. Now I pressed my body against hers. I could smell her lipstick, its thick aroma. I moved in to kiss her. She backed away a little. I grabbed her little waist and pulled her in. She smiled, then dropped her smile completely and looked deeply at me, like the tide getting sucked in on the shore before getting smashed by waves. Now our lips met, full open-mouthed kisses, our tongues touching and caressing. We both stopped dancing, our bodies slowly melding, sliding up and down each other. The lights were flashing, the beat was pounding. My entire being was absorbed in a feeling, as if my mind was now just the colors on the dance floor.

The music stopped. Miriam and I remained on the dance floor, kissing, holding hands tightly.

We were both jolted out of the spell by Tommy and Martha speaking to us.

"Look at you two," said Tommy. "You're like little love bunnies." Tommy and Martha held hands, too. But Miriam and I were beside ourselves.

"You want to walk to the park?" asked Tommy.

I looked at Miriam and nodded yes.

The fresh air felt silky on my face. The streets were wet, the rain making them slick and dark blue. We all walked on the street together, two couples holding hands.

Tommy walked ahead with Martha. I stopped every now and then, giving Miriam deep tongue kisses.

"Come on, love birds," Tommy called after us when we lagged behind.

We both walked quickly to catch up.

Once at the park, we sat on the benches separately and made out. The night was growing blacker by the minute, like it was disappearing. All I could hear was the sound of Miriam's lips meeting mine.

I looked up at the stars feeling that they glittered for me, for us. The cool breeze and the stars were ours.

I kissed Miriam again.

"What are you thinking?" she asked.

I didn't know what to say, how to say it.

She shoved me. "Come on, tell me."

"I'm thinking about you, how beautiful you are and how great this night has been."

"Oh, that's so sweet," she said.

What I was really thinking was that the stars might never look the same again, that maybe they'd lose their twinkle and would forever be dull empty dots in the sky. This breeze, this shade of dark blue would never happen again. So, I reached out and held Miriam's face. I looked long and deep in her eyes. I hadn't yet noticed that they were slightly grey blue. They sparkled in the lamppost light. I took in a breath and drank in her fragrance then I kissed her like it was the last kiss I'd ever get, like my life depended on it.

NO STRINGS ATTACHED

Months after I stopped taking lessons at Debellis Music, I still stopped by to buy guitar strings and check out their new guitars. I bantered with Mike Debellis. Mike worked behind the counter. His family owned the business.

"Have you tried these D'Addario strings?" asked Mike, chewing gum. He wore sunglasses on his head, his forehead matted by locks of brown hair. Mike handed me the package of strings. I was mesmerized by the bright and colorful packaging; they looked like something made of gems.

He stared at me for a moment after he stopped speaking.

"Hey, would you be interested in trying out for a band?" he then asked.

"Me?" I replied dumbly.

"Our guitar player just quit. You look like you can play."

"I can play."

"What kind of stuff do you play?"

"Rock music, you know, Led Zeppelin, Hendrix."

"We play ballads," he said. "But we can rock. We're looking to cut a demo tape, get a contract. Can you read music?"

"Not really," I said. "I can read chords. I have a good ear."

"Didn't you take lessons here?" he said, cork-screwing his nose.

"I took some lessons," I replied, a little defensively.

"And you don't know how to read music?"

"Not really."

"That's okay," he said, shrugging. "The guitar stuff isn't really complicated."

"Where do I go for the tryout?" I asked.

"We rehearse here—at the store. Come down, Wednesday at 8 PM."

I turned to go away.

"You don't have to bring a guitar," he said, pointing to the wall of electric guitars. "You can use one of these." Hanging from the rack was a sunburst red Gibson Les Paul, a Flying V and a bone white Fender Stratocaster, like Hendrix played.

I left the store mulling over what Mike said. They were looking to cut a demo tape, get a music contract. I was excited. I was still young enough to believe that maybe I could be a rock star.

I started playing guitar when I was about fourteen, inspired by images and sounds of rock music. The dragon roar of Jimmy Page's Heartbreaker solo. The Valkyrie shrieks of Plant's vocals. Santana, the Who. Meaty Beaty Big and Bouncy. The psychedelic album covers. The guitar shapes and burning colors. Coming from a drab working-class industrial section of Queens, rock music was like a mysterious call from mythological beings. I had to learn to play guitar.

After practicing for about six months, I achieved forty percent of the soloing guitar skill I have today at fifty-two. Practicing with my best friend, Lan, we played extensive jams, emulating our heroes, like Cream, Hendrix and Zeppelin. We weren't afraid to play badly, or loudly, and sometimes we even sounded okay. And all of this playing and listening occurred in a chamber of marijuana smoke. Pot helped elevate my listening to music; it also supplied the trapdoor I needed to escape the deadened steel factory prison of Long Island City. While smoking weed may have offered transport to a fairytale land, it also enabled me to hide behind a cumulus wall. I could fail at everything and blame it on the pot smoking. If I didn't do anything, I could always wrap myself up in a blanket of smoke to feel better. Pot was a cloud I could take cover in, get lost and find myself in, like an Aztec maze.

As we started to play more and more, I realized I needed some guitar lessons. That's how I found Debellis Music on Broadway, near where I lived. My assigned teacher, Jim, was only a few years older. Jim taught me some basic scales, bar chords and some fingerpicking technique. I also sold an ounce of weed for him. But, after about a year, I stopped going to music lessons. I stopped because studying music was work; I just wanted to play. I instead used the money my father had given me to buy pot.

Then, at about sixteen, after going to a school counselor, knowing I was spinning around on a carousel to nowhere, I stopped smoking pot. With the cloud lifted, I began to see who I really was: an insecure kid, uncertain of myself. I'd spent nights on the stairs of our project building waiting to come down from a high so I could confront my parents. I'd hung out with some crazy tough guys who were intent on killing themselves. Then I stopped hanging out with reckless lunatics. And now I was trying to attempt things without a crutch, or a shield. If I failed, it would be my failure.

I showed up to the rehearsal at Debellis Music a little nervous.

Mike introduced me to the band.

"This is Jeff, the bass player." Jeff was tall and nerdy looking. His lanky body curved, like he was made of rubber. He smoked cigarettes holding them backwards between his thumb and forefinger, like a European.

"And this is Matt, the piano player," added Mike. Matt wore horn-rimmed glasses and looked like an engineer. "Matt writes the music to all of the songs."

We talked a little bit about the music we liked. Jeff was into New Wave groups like Devo, the Cars, but studied jazz and could read music. Matt was a classically trained piano player. I felt a little self-conscious. They were knowledgeable and serious. And they were all older than I was, by a few years. How was I going to be able to hold my own?

Then they played one of the songs they had written. We were only going to perform original songs. The song was called "Now Love Begins." Mike sang vocals. He wasn't very good. The song was a little corny, but it was catchy. The piano and bass parts were interesting. It was a little like smooth jazz.

"Can you play along this time?" asked Mike. "Which guitar do you want?"

I walked over to the row of guitars, pulling the Fender Stratocaster off of the hook.

Mike then placed the sheet music for piano in front of me.

"I don't know the chords," I said, a little embarrassed.

"That's okay," said Matt, taking my guitar with his left hand. With his right hand he played chords on the keyboard. Then he wrote the chords down on a piece of paper. They were jazz chords, sevenths, major-sevenths and so forth. Not what I typically played.

He handed me the paper.

"Let's try now," said Mike.

I strummed along hesitantly, as Matt galloped through the opening verses.

"Like this?" I asked.

"You can give it more swing," offered Jeff.

I picked up the rhythm, alternating on up and down strokes.

"Now, there's a guitar solo part here," said Mike. "That's what Tony used to do, at least." He paused. "You don't have to."

"I'll give it a try," I said. "What key?"

"It's in A minor," said Matt. "You can play the C major scale over it."

When Lan and I used to play, I soloed for up to five minutes sometimes, like my guitar heroes Clapton, Alvin Lee and Hendrix. Even if we weren't very good, we played with exuberance. Our playing was charged and athletic. All of this poured out in the seconds that followed. As if a light bulb went on, my soloing caught fire, with a mix of rapid trills and bluesy pull-offs. But this stretch only lasted for a few brief moments; then I suddenly became scared and backed off. Like I was caught dreaming out loud.

Then we practiced on a few improvised blues songs. It was clear that I was more comfortable improvising. Afterwards, they rehearsed a few more of their songs. I played along after hearing them a few times. One of their songs, "First Class Love Trip," had a tricky time signature and I struggled through the chords. Despite this, the songs sounded okay. They were very good musicians, and what I lacked in knowledge and skill, I made up for in willingness. Overall, though, I felt that I didn't fit into the band's style. They were more like a wedding band. I was like a hot pistol dropped on a dance floor, randomly shooting bullets.

"Sorry, that was kind of a train wreck," I said, after the song, knowing I missed some of the changes.

"It was rough," said Mike. "But it was good."

"Really?"

"It was good," added Jeff.

I wasn't convinced. But appreciated the feedback. I was sunk into the notion that I wasn't very good, and they were better musicians. I saw everything from that perspective.

"I need to go to the bathroom," I said. When I looked at the clock, I realized we'd been playing for three hours.

"You know where it is," said Mike. "You've been here before."

When I came back it was like I interrupted their talking.

"It's late, we should call it a night," said Mike. "Tryout is over."

I unplugged the Stratocaster and hung it back on the wall, knowing I didn't play well enough.

"So, what are you doing next Wednesday?" asked Mike.

I shrugged.

"Want to come to rehearsal?"

"Do you mean to try out again?"

"No, I mean rehearsal. You made the band." He looked at the other guys. "That is, if you'd like to be in the band."

"Well, wow, let me think about it," I said, stunned. "I mean, of course I'd like to be in the band."

"How old are you, by the way?" asked Mike.

"I'm sixteen," I said.

"See," said Mike, adding "I told you he was a few years younger than us. He's a kid." He chuckled and then we all laughed a little along with him.

"So, am I still in?" I asked.

"You got something there with that playing. It's a little rough, but I can mold you."

I just looked at him; I wasn't sure if this was a compliment, or what.

"See you next week," said Mike.

In the months that followed, I attended every rehearsal. The band actually started to sound good. I continued to see myself as the weakest link, even though they all supported and encouraged me. I was adapting to the style, taming my heavy-handed rock guitar playing. Also, now Tom had joined the group, as the drummer. Tom was attending our rehearsals, bringing a rock sensibility to the group, slightly more akin to my playing.

Mike Debellis was not only the leader of the group; he was also the primary singer. While he wasn't very good, he enabled us to use the store for rehearsals and instruments. And he kept talking about the demo tape we were going to record. And Mike seemed to be our promoter, talking to agents and contacts about potential shows and even a record contract, he said.

"I've booked us to play at a high school in Long Island," said Mike, as if that was impressive. This is where our tour would kick off. We didn't yet have any other dates scheduled.

"We're going to be big," added Mike. Matt, Jeff, Tom and I nodded in agreement. None of us had either the courage or the heart to say anything otherwise.

Privately, Jeff and I met and played together. Jeff's apartment wasn't very far from me. We played rock songs and extended blues progressions. I looked up to Jeff; he knew more about music than I did. I was everyone's understudy, the kid in the band.

"Mike's full of shit with that 'we're going to be a star' crap," said Jeff, wedging his cigarette between strings on his bass, a cool rock musician trick.

"I know," I said. "He sucks as a singer, too."

"His sister can sing, though."

"She's great. I wish Mike sang like her," I said.

"She's going to come to more rehearsals, I hear. Along with Greg." Greg sometimes came to our rehearsals. Greg was a natural musician. He played piano and guitar and sang harmonies. He had long hair, like a hippie. He was studying music and film at New York University. Greg came from a world I wanted to be in.

"They're going to make up for Mike's shitty singing," said Jeff. "Hopefully they'll just sing over him."

We both laughed.

As the weeks went by, we were all excited about the upcoming studio session, the scheduled performance date and other performances that would come. Things were looking up.

When we arrived at the studio to cut the demo tape, everyone was dressed up, like we were going out to a party, since Mike wanted to take promotional pictures, too. The pictures would be on the jacket of the album, he said. I wore white Capezio shoes, since they were the fanciest shoes I owned. Everyone laughed at me, except for Amy, Mike's sister. When she said "They look cute on you" and looked me up and down, it sent a chill up my spine.

We didn't have a lot of time, so we played the songs a few times over and recorded each take. I was very nervous, afraid that I'd make a mistake that would ruin the demo tape. I kept apologizing to everyone.

We took a break at the half-point of the day. While the engineer, Adel, was mixing the recording, I was in one of the back rooms making out with Amy. This was bound to happen, as she'd been flirting with me at the past few rehearsals. I hoped Mike wouldn't be upset at me for fooling around with his sister.

"Okay, now it's your turn in the booth," said Adel. "For the solos."

I wiped my mouth with my shirt, trying to remove any trace of Amy's hot pink glossy lipstick. The fragrance of the lipstick lingered on my own lips.

I took a deep breath and picked up the Fender Stratocaster that I'd borrowed from the store. I was slightly emboldened by the hot kissing I'd been doing in the backroom with Amy and also a little bit embarrassed.

I walked into the soundproof booth, put on the earphones and sat on a stool.

Adel talked to me through the flicking switches on the board.

"Okay, we'll do one take and then try a cut," he said.

"Ready when you are."

The music started, I waited for my part. I played an improvised solo, as I had always done. I followed the melody in my solo, adding some flourishes, unable to completely suppress my rock guitar sensibility.

"That was a good take," said Adel. "Now, we're going to do a real take."

The song started again. I adjusted myself on the stool, crossing my right leg over my left leg. This time, I felt better. I started playing, looking at everyone through the glass window. I was digging into the melody, bending the strings. It sounded good to me. The engineer, Adel, pumped his fist toward me as I played. Mike and the others cheered me on, like I'd just hit a fly ball that was heading toward the bleachers.

On that stool, I felt like I was perched high above the ground, like an eagle sitting on a branch at the top of a tall tree, seeing everything around me. I wasn't self-conscious. I was lifted by the moment to a rarified place, like my moorings were unattached. I was floating high above the Long Island City factory buildings, soaring into the clouds. I was high. Very high. But mostly, I was high without smoking pot.

Days later, at rehearsal, Mike produced a tape of the recordings. Now Amy attended the rehearsals. She'd even sing some of the songs with Mike. As we gathered around to hear the recording, Amy sat next to me. We held hands. I was a little embarrassed to be so public about our affections.

"Be good to my sister," said Mike, raising an eyebrow as he wagged a finger at me. He was half-joking.

When Mike walked away, Jeff whispered, "Hey, because of you, we have a real singer coming to our rehearsals now."

Now our focus was on the show in Long Island. Mike talked it up like we were playing at Carnegie Hall. It wasn't even a paid gig; it was at a high school.

Not sure if it was my inner cynic, but I felt that things could only go downhill from here. I never said a word about it to anyone, not even Jeff. I just didn't believe that good things could happen for me.

I was nervous the night of the Long Island show. When we arrived, I saw the stage we'd perform on. It didn't look like a stage where a rock band would play. It looked like a place where talent shows took place.

The performance itself is a fog to me now. All I can remember is that we didn't play the songs terribly well. Despite the miscues, Mike strutted and pranced, like a peacock. The wide cuffs of his shirt were rolled up to his wrists. His shirt was unbuttoned, the hair on his chest exposed. A gold cross lay on a bed of chest hair, like it was giving comfort to the crucified Christ.

In the weeks that followed, I learned that I received a scholarship to attend New York University. All of my attention was directed to that. I had visions of going to school in the Village, hanging out with cool looking people, discussing philosophy and literature. Only a few years ago, I'd hung out in Washington Square Park smoking pot, inhaling nitrous oxide and trying to cop mescaline. Now, I would walk through the park proudly, as a student. I wouldn't be just a street kid looking up at the campus buildings. I'd be walking their hallways, sitting in their classrooms.

I missed a few rehearsals, feeling bad that I was abandoning the band, that I was breaking the spell of Mike's dream. I didn't call Amy either.

The summer was nearing an end. As the weeks drifted by, I lost all intentions of returning to rehearsals, or calling Amy. My sights were set on the future that awaited me. It didn't include playing with the band. We didn't even have a name.

But I had the recordings on tape. Even now, I take the tape out (now converted to CD and also copied to my iTunes playlist), listen to the songs and recall that, in practicing them, I was saving myself. I feel bad that I never called Mike, or anyone else. I feel terrible that I just split the scene.

All that remains are the songs. They are echoes from a past. They're not so bad. And the guitar playing is pretty good. I hear Amy's voice soaring above the keyboard notes. The music remains placed high on a misted mountain peak. I can still feel the flight of that solo. When I hear the song, I can still see the azure blue of the sky I was reeling in.

ROLLER ROYCE

I'd met Gina Ricaboni at one of Mike Ferrone's house parties. When I say parties, they were more like gatherings where sixteen-year-olds got wasted and snuck into rooms to make out and grope. Getting into each other's pants was always a plus.

When I met Gina she looked different than most of the other neighborhood girls. She hardly wore any makeup, except for a little lip gloss. And her clothes weren't flashy. She dressed like she'd just come from a tennis lesson.

"I've seen you at Party Palace," I said, knowing she lived near there, trying to find a way to talk to her. Party Palace was tucked into the back section of PS 210. We called it Party Palace because kids would go there to get stoned, hang out and drink beer. The red brick walls were marked with sprawling graffiti. Kids pissed in the corners, the same place where they crushed their cigarettes and beer cans. And the same place where they made out.

"I've been there," said Gina, curtly. She spoke clearly. She didn't talk like she had rocks in her mouth. In our neighborhood, speaking without a harsh accent stood out. It was like those who articulated their words and who fully opened their mouths when they spoke were being fancy. But I was in love with the way Gina spoke, although I didn't know why. Her whole being emanated illumination. Even Gina's eyes were bright and alive. She was confident, unlike me. I feigned confidence. I was not yet conscious of why I lacked confidence.

"What were you doing there?" I asked with a wink and a smile, trying to break the impenetrable puss on her face. No one went to Party Palace to just hang out.

"Nothing really," she said. Her face remained stoic. Her emerald green eyes glowed like gems. I knew her cousins who lived near the park. She had just moved from Riverdale to Long Island City. I'd heard that her father had passed away from a heart attack, so her mother moved back to be closer to family. Her mother had left Long Island City many years before, in the sixties, when she'd gone to college.

"But I saw you there with your friends, Ferrone and Squitelli," she added in a mocking tone. She rubbed one index finger over the other. "Tsk tsk tsk."

I froze for a minute, like my secrets had been exposed. Seen. Like someone knew more about me than I told them. I did a lot of bad shit with those guys. Got into fights, sniffed glue. Shit I wasn't proud of.

When she realized she had the upper hand, she finally smiled. It was like a thousand birds just swirled across the sky. She was so pretty.

For a moment, I must have looked like a thief caught in the act, but then I relaxed with a smirk on my face.

"Now that you know my secrets," I said, "how would you like to meet Saturday night at Roller Royce?"

"You mean the skating rink?"

"The one near Ditmars, under the el."

She took a step back, brought her hand up to her face and chuckled.

"What?" I asked, looking around to see if anyone saw her laughing.

"It's just that," she paused, bit her upper lip, then looked at me blinking, as if holding back another guffaw.

"Well?"

"You're asking me on a date, right?"

I nodded yes. "Why is that so funny?" My voice cracked a little.

"Well, it's just that it's a goofy place. I mean, I would never just go there."

"Here's your chance then; you could blame it on me and say I dragged you there," I replied, trying to stand up straight and tall.

Still grinning, she paused for a moment.

"It's fun. I've been there once before," I added, lying. I'd been there a bunch of times. I went to Roller Royce to pick up girls, get high, and gawp at the colorful flashing lights.

Gina now stared at me, like she was studying me. I couldn't figure it out then. Thinking back now, I know why she was looking at me this way.

"Come on, you'll have a great time, I promise," I said. It sounded like I was pleading now.

"Okay," she finally answered, letting out a sigh. I didn't care that her answer sounded more like an act of charity than anything else.

We then made plans to meet that Friday night. Saying goodbye, I leaned in to give her a hug and she shoved her hand at me to shake. It wasn't a cool handshake. It was cold and formal. I cautiously shook her hand, my palm only slightly sliding into hers. Our fingers didn't touch.

That Friday night, I changed my clothes about three times before I left my house. Should I dress more like a rocker or a disco guy I wondered? I wasn't sure which she'd like more.

I decided not to wear my dungaree jacket. I wore slacks with my Capezios. While guys always made fun of my Capezios, girls seemed to like them. It was like I had style.

I arrived at Roller Royce a few minutes before seven, our agreed time. I wanted to make sure I didn't look sweaty or disheveled. I ran my fingers down the crease of my white gabardine pants. I double checked my pearly white Capezios to make sure there were no scuff marks on them.

Since it was summer, the sun was still shining brightly. It wasn't a hot night. The air was smooth and light.

Gina arrived just a little after seven. She looked beautiful. Her dark hair was wrapped in a tight bun. Her eyes glimmered from the sparkle makeup she wore. Her lips glistened from pink lipstick. She had white shorts on that showed her legs.

As I leaned toward her to give her a hug, again, she shoved her hand at me. No one in my neighborhood shook hands like that, much less the girls I knew.

She looked me up and down.

"Nice shoes," she said, snickering.

"You like them?"

"They're funny in a cute way."

"Funny?" I asked. That wasn't the effect I'd hoped they'd have.

"They're fine. Perfect for Roller Royce," she added.

We went to the front desk to rent our skates and get our locker keys, then met back on the rink.

I looked up at the multicolored lights. The ceiling looked like the hull of a gigantic spaceship. The flickering lights ricocheted off of spinning glitter balls that dangled from the top of the arena. The alternating lights and colors pumped to the beat of "Funkytown." As we floated into the rink, we both gawked up at the dizzying spectacle of lights.

I reached out to hold Gina's hand. Not to shake it, but to hold it. To caress it. She looked at my hand like I had a knife in it. My hand hung suspended in the air for what felt like an eternity. I wasn't used to this kind of rejection. I made out with girls from my neighborhood at places like Party Palace after only having just met them. It was easy. Not like this.

My hand still out, she finally clapped her hand on mine, and we swooshed into the rink. The floors were wooden, our wheels clanging on the hard floor, like prison chains.

Now that we were skating, we couldn't talk much. The pounding of the music and the pulsing lights made us have to mime our conversation. I made faces, lifting one foot up, twirling a little, and showing off some tricks I'd learned. She mirrored my gestures. Her moves were measured and small, as she hadn't done them before. The entire time, she smiled and laughed. They weren't mocking laughs, like the one about my Capezios. I could tell she was having a good time. We held hands. Our fingers now sometimes coiling around each other.

On most other nights, I would have had a beer, or two, or smoked a joint. But not tonight. I didn't want to show up stoned to meet Gina. I knew I had to pay attention. I couldn't just laugh everything off. She was too fast for me. Too much ahead of every move.

Towards the end of the night, the DJ played Donna Summer's "Last Dance." At this point, I'd usually be making out heavily with the girl I was with. Maybe we'd finish the night at Party Palace, gliding our bodies up against each other in one of its dark corners.

As the lush piano notes of "Last Dance" bounced off the arena walls, Gina rolled her eyes. Of course, I hated the song too.

Tilting my head, pursing my lips, as if to say, yes, I too loathe this song, but we must do this, I again reached out my hand to her. This time, she readily took it.

Then I placed my hands on her waist. Gina gently wound her arms around my neck. As the song played, we looked into each other's eyes. She smiled. I smiled. I wanted to kiss her but wouldn't risk the injury of a rejection. She looked at my lips. I looked at hers; they were pink and moist. She had probably slyly applied gloss again when I wasn't looking. As "Last Dance" broke out of the ballad intro, we started to dance in our skates.

Then I walked Gina back to her three-story house, near PS 210. Still holding hands, we talked about our favorite books. About music that we liked. It was a quiet summer night. The sky was clear. You could even see a few stars, which was uncommon for Long Island City. The moon glowed overhead, showering us with silver light as we walked along the cement streets.

"So, this is where I live," said Gina, pointing to her house.

"Nice house," I said, looking up.

"It's not like our house in Riverdale, but it's okay."

I didn't want to mention anything about her father's heart attack or say anything to make her upset. I just wanted to kiss her.

"I had fun," I said.

"Me too."

"Maybe we can do this again some time?"

"Yeah, maybe," she offered.

I lingered, trying to find a way to give her a kiss.

She tapped her foot, bit her upper lip, gripping the handles on her pocketbook, curling them up into her hands.

"Well, I guess this is goodnight," I said.

"Goodnight. And thanks," she said.

Before I could lean in to give her a hug, she shot her hand out at me to shake.

I looked at her hand for a moment, then let go a smile. We shook hands.

At that moment, I knew I'd never see her again. And I never did.

TOM TURKEY'S TIE DYE

Tom Turkey wears a tie-dyed shirt and loose-fitting yoga pants; his long blond hair hangs in dreadlocks down his back. He is tanned, like he spent the summer trekking through the Mexican Baja, meditating with shamans.

My friend Ivan and I sit on a bench in Ravenswood smoking weed with Tom Turkey and Dakota, his girlfriend. Dakota is thumbing through a paperback copy of *Leaves of Grass*, reading passages out loud. The cover of the book is bedecked in bright green leaves.

"Keep your face always toward the sunshine and shadows will fall behind you," says Dakota, reciting Whitman, with a slight lisp, slowly enunciating each word.

Dakota sits cross-legged on the bench with *Leaves* perched in her hand. Despite her hippie dress, her long thin legs manage to escape into view. As I listen to her words, I am thinking about how smooth and perfect her legs are. Her skin is like the white contours of bleached sand dunes. Dakota doesn't wear any makeup, yet her perfect lips glisten a light pink hue.

"Hey man," says Tom Turkey to Ivan and me, stroking the braids of his long hair, "I got Suns and I'll give them to you for three dollars apiece, but each of you have to take six hits now." Ivan's been talking about taking acid all summer.

Neither Ivan nor I respond to Turkey's dare.

Now turning away from us, Turkey takes out a dulcimer from the case slung over his shoulder. The dulcimer has miniature rune carvings on it and faces of wood nymphs. As he strums, plucking out *Lord of the Rings*-like melodies, he stops and schools us about the LSD he has.

"I risk a lot transporting this back from California," he says, then continues strumming.

"It's too good to sell to just anyone. I don't want to waste these on amateurs."

Now Turkey puts down the dulcimer to light a bowl of weed. The bowl, too, is decorated with runes, like he bought the dulcimer and bowl as a set. Dragging on the bowl like he's sucking air from a hole in the ground just to stay alive, he lets out a massive plume. I imagine that he'd be able to exhale smoke into tree-nymph and fairy shapes, like Gandalf did in *Lord of the Rings*.

"Of course, if you don't want them," says Turkey, his voice trailing off. He hands the bowl to Ivan. Ivan has a big crooked nose, bad teeth, and long scraggly hair. Whereas Turkey is suave and handsome in his hippie-dippy outfit, Ivan looks like Magwitch from *Great Expectations*. We call Ivan "Spare Parts" because he looks like he was assembled from discarded parts in a machine shop. One arm is jammed in the socket; the other arm shorter and slightly curved at the elbow. Buck teeth hammered into his gums, like tombstones.

Emerging from his wordless chrysalis, Ivan looks up, finally, saying "We'll take them," inhaling smoke from the bowl. As he coughs, he nods at me for agreement. "These are the Suns I've been telling you about," says Ivan. "This isn't like the shitty acid you get in Washington Square Park. This is Owsley acid," he says, like he knows. That summer I'd read *Doors of Perception* and *The Electric Kool-Aid Acid Test*, preparing for an epic psychedelic trip. I had even taken half a tab of blotter acid a few weeks ago. But six hits? Ivan said that he'd felt the beating-heart center of Cygnus X-1 tripping on six hits of acid. He also told me he took acid every day a few years ago but then had to stop. "I started to get creepy, started losing my mind." And I can't imagine him any more insane than he already is.

As I sit there on the park bench, swinging my feet back and forth, I think of what's ahead of me. Next fall I'll attend college. Taking acid is my pre-college workshop, like summer school with Timothy Leary.

"I'll do it, too," I say to Turkey.

Turkey hands us the Sun hits and we give him our money. We immediately take the acid, letting the paper melt on our tongues. It's tasteless.

In the shade of the trees, the light summer breeze sprays a soft tapping of kisses on my face. We are all stoned now from the weed. Turkey again starts plucking his dulcimer as Dakota sings in a high-pitched voice, accompanying him. The words of the song describe ancient humans taking hallucinogens. The world was in order and perfect at that time, the song suggests. Believing all of this crap, I'm getting tingles down my spine. Their voices sound pretty good together. I'm quietly wondering why we can't go back to being perfect storybook creatures, having achieved cosmic balance and harmony with the universe.

When they stop playing, Turkey reminds us that he's the grandchild of Aldous Huxley. He's said this shit before.

"My father moved from England in the fifties to get away from the Huxley name," Turkey says.

"Grandpa Aldous used to read *The Tibetan Book of the Dead* to me when I was a baby."

I don't believe Turkey, but I'm stoned and want to believe him. I imagine him in a baby genie outfit as Grandpa Aldous rocks him to sleep.

The truth of the matter is that I'm jealous of Turkey. I'd like to travel the world with a beautiful woman, searching for shamans and wisdom teachers. Instead, the closest I have to a wisdom teacher is my slightly deformed and satanic friend, Ivan.

As the acid courses into my bloodstream, I see a light dalliance of colors shining off of the trees, the bench and swelling up from the ground. I start playing with the antenna on a radio I hadn't noticed. It has been silent the whole time, as if spying on us. As the antenna flickers back and forth, it splashes a spectrum of rainbow colors.

"I can see the waves," I say aloud. Ivan laughs.

Now that the acid is taking effect, Turkey gets restless. He didn't want to hang out with a bunch of amateurs; he just wanted to make sure that we had taken the acid. For a goof.

As I turn to look at Turkey, I am transfixed by Dakota's dress. I can't see her long sexy legs anymore. Her dress is roaring with color; it's rippling like a Mexican sunset, the streaks of yellow engulfing streaks of pink.

Acid makes me talk out loud for some reason. I begin describing the hallucinations I am having.

"This is like the River Styx," I say, pointing at a long rivulet of color, my pupils as big and wet as giant goldfish. "This purple band is gurgling lava."

Now Dakota laughs at me. I'm completely serious. I want to impress her. Maybe Turkey recites *The Tibetan Book of the Dead* to her. He speaks like a T.S. Eliot poem. I'm sure Turkey is wise when he tells her about his cosmic visions. I'm sure she sees me the way I see Ivan, an ugly moron.

"We have to get going," says Tom Turkey.

I don't want Dakota to leave, whether she likes me or feels sorry for me. And I am convinced she'll make sure my trip goes well. Being left alone with Ivan could turn out badly.

"Happy trails," says Turkey, "wherever your airplane happens to land." At that moment, I hate Turkey. How could she go out with him? Doesn't she realize that he's a fucking phony? And that bullshit about being Huxley's grandson.

Turkey takes Dakota by the hand and slings the dulcimer case over his shoulder, like he's galloping off into the sunset. Seeing the sadness in my eyes, Dakota takes a step towards me and leans over to give me a kiss and muss my hair. Her lips touch my cheek. Even though her kiss is like a big sister's, the sensation sends rushes across my body, like I've been touched by lightning. The kiss ricochets across nerve endings, rumbles in my guts and prickles my scalp, exploding finally in my fingertips and toes.

Snapping out of my daydream, I shake my head.

"How will the airplane take you home?" I ask. I didn't mean to say that.

Dakota and Turkey giggle.

Walking away, Dakota starts waving goodbye. Even down the block I can see her still waving. It is like a game we're playing. I keep waving until she is the size of a baseball. As she continues walking, I see that now she's only a wavy line. Even when she disappears, I see her as a swirl of pink in the distance. I don't know how long this game has gone on for. I start to cry. I'll never meet a woman like her. The tears pour down my face like runoff from a river. I turn away.

Wiping the tears from my face, I look to see if Ivan notices. He doesn't.

Now Ivan and I are alone.

The acid is shooting through my veins now. The ground sparkles with a rainbow shimmer. Even the little rocks on the ground are speckled with diamonds. The leaves on the trees are so bright they look like they will explode into a million tiny pieces. I see visual memes of the *Leaves of Grass* book cover everywhere: on the trees, on the ground, in the sky.

"Let's go to Roosevelt Island," says Ivan. Roosevelt Island has parks and trees. The East River flows between the Island and Manhattan. I signal agreement, my head bobbling back and forth, like I am a wooden puppet, incapable of using words.

We walk down to Rainey Park, then onto the bridge that takes us to Roosevelt Island. I am hallucinating visions of stories being told in the surface of the water far below us. It is like a continuation of the mythic tales that Turkey and Dakota had talked about. I wish Dakota was walking hand in hand with me.

The face of Poseidon forms on the water surface below. As Poseidon speaks to us, I ask Ivan if he can also see Poseidon.

"Yes, I see him," he says. "He wants to eat your brains." That's not what I want to hear.

"Fuck you, you're just making that shit up," I say. Ivan cracks a sinister smile. His long scraggly hair is combed over one side of his head, like he's a fugitive from the Manson family.

Soon my stomach starts to feel nauseous. My insides are swishing around, like I swallowed a snake.

The sun's rays are now pounding down on us as if poured from a waterfall. I am sweating profusely. With each pump of fresh blood to my heart, the acid rushes through my bloodstream with a dizzying intensity.

Six hits? And from Turkey? I should have known better.

"You know Poseidon is a minion of Satan," says Ivan, contorting his face, bulging his left eyeball. It's completely red.

"I'm not feeling so well so shut the fuck up, man," I say. "I think the acid was too strong."

We keep walking, but I have to stop. I sit down on a bench hyperventilating.

"Let's go home," I say.

"You can never go home."

"Either we go home," I say, "or I'm going to the emergency room."

Now my body begins shutting down, the acid arresting my senses. The sun is too big for me; it's everywhere in the sky. Like an egg that has leaked its yolk, the sun's heat is dripping on me, heavy, syrupy. I'm holding my chest, breathing heavily.

Seeing me squirm on the bench, Ivan finally agrees to go home.

Walking in the heat, my head feels round like an overflowing fishbowl; my heart racing like it will jump out of my chest. I now see pits of hell with demon-faced monsters peering out of them. I put my hands over my face trying not to see demon countenances. But the monsters emerge from the darkness of my hands. Visions of death all around me. Dogs hanging from lampposts. Charred bodies of eyeless children. The grinning faces of devils. Their eye sockets running with blood, spiders pouring out from their apertures.

"We're almost home," says Ivan, knowing that I'm in bad shape. "Don't worry, you'll be fine." Even though he's an asshole, he knows I could fall off the face of the earth without his help. And he'd have to answer to someone for it. The cops, my parents. Who knows?

When we finally get to his house, I am relieved to be out of the sun. We couldn't have gone to my house. I look haunted, like a zombie, pale and frightened. My parents would have called a doctor. Or an exorcist.

Now in his bedroom, Ivan puts on music. He leaves me alone and as I lie on his bed, the ceiling erupts like an upside-down volcano.

He returns with a pitcher full of red Kool-Aid. The color and consistency of the liquid are soothing. I drink the Kool-Aid down in long gulps. The sweetness of the drink eases my brain, like I'm drinking a river of easy-going forever redness. The dimness of the room feels good. The sun is out there, but it's only seeping in from the cracks in the shades, not blaring down on us like an angry god.

My central nervous system slows down like I'm on the local and not the express train to hell anymore. The walls heave and shrink, but gracefully. The walls are like a gigantic cinematic screen. The entire history of the universe is being played out before my eyes. But it's not just visual, it's emotional. Simultaneously, I'm crying about the birth of our sun and the formation of the galaxies. I feel sad that my parents still live in the Ravenswood Projects.

"See," Ivan says.

"See what?"

"See how cool it is."

"Yeah, it's cool."

"But you wigged out, man."

"It was all your fault," I say. "You're a fucking maniac. What's with all of the Satan talk?"

"I like being in the belly of the beast," he says. "You don't learn anything from the good trips."

"Well, I don't need to learn anything. Leave me alone with that shit."

As I take another slug of the Kool-Aid, the music smoothly races around my brain. My thoughts are like hamsters on a wheel.

"This is here all of the time," says Ivan. "We just can't see it. But the ancients could see this shit," he says passing me a joint.

This is, like, how the Mayans lived, I think to myself. The Mayans took hallucinogens, looked up into the skies and could see into the future. These trips bridge you to another reality, another time and place, like Turkey said. All you have to do is take these little pieces of paper and you're projected into another realm.

"The music holds the secrets too," I say, philosophizing and talking shit. "It's like everyone who takes this shit can read the messages in the music." Everywhere is a portal to another world.

"We can do this again," says Ivan.

"No fucking talk about demons."

"Okay, no demons next time. But you're missing out man."

"Don't be a fucking asshole, okay?"

As I sit across from this unhinged mutant, no longer beating back a sea of demons, I know that I have peered outside of the little world that has bounded my experience.

As fucked up as Ivan is, he has opened up a door. Having gone first to hell, my mind is leaning into the sunshine. Beyond our glorious sun, I see the spirals of the Milky Way. And this is only the beginning. The universe is boundless. I'll go wherever my airplane takes me.

HIRED TODAY

When we went to apply for the doorman job, my brother Virgil and I were quickly ushered past the line of Black men and women who were waiting to fill out applications and sent directly to the hiring manager's office. All union hotel workers were on strike.

A bald white man in glasses pointed to us and said, "Hire them."

That day we were given light brown doorman suits with green stripes and walked out to face the strikers. As soon as we swung open the heavy glass doors of the air-conditioned hotel, we were met with the clamor of the crowd. The screams mingled with gusts of heat, blanketing us, sucking the oxygen out of the air.

They were only about a hundred feet away on the sidewalk, chanting "HIRED TODAY, FIRED TOMORROW," over and over. The strikers alternated this chant with "NO HOUSEKEEPING, NO SECURITY."

The workers shook signs at us that said "GO HOME SCABBIES." They were from the Caribbean, from South America, from Africa, even from the Bronx and Brooklyn. They were maintenance men, housekeepers and security guards. They were like the people I had grown up with, hardworking, with kind round faces. Some worked late-night shifts, going home at six in the morning. Some worked into the night, leaving at eleven in the evening.

My parents were adamant about it. "If you want to go to college you have to work during the strike." I didn't fully understand what a strike was about.

The previous year, when I was nineteen and in my second year of college, Virgil and I had worked at The Berkshire Hotel on Madison Avenue and 51st Street as doormen and elevator operators. Prior to hotels, I'd worked as a deli counterperson, a dishwasher at a restaurant and a maintenance man at a women's clothing store.

But I didn't know the details of a union strike. I had read about them in newspapers and in history books. It's one thing to read about a strike, it's another thing to be embroiled in the center of the chaos. To make matters worse, the union wanted this strike more than the workers. I was on the side of workers. The workers wanted their jobs. Going on strike meant losing pay; if they didn't go on strike, their livelihoods would be jeopardized. The workers arrived to strike with all this anguish.

Until the day I showed up to work as a scab, I didn't know that people would be howling at me for eight hours until their eyes filled with tears of disgust. A doorman doesn't only see the strikers as he enters and exits a hotel; he's their kicking post for eight hours a day. None of us knew that the people would get so heated they'd even throw explosives at us.

Virgil worked the 8 AM shift. I started my eight-hour shift at eleven in the morning. For the first two hours, the strikers were quiet, eating breakfast, assembling. By the time I arrived, the crowd had thickened, the pitch of the chants had increased. Our shifts overlapped and then Virgil left a few hours before I did.

Even in the first few days, the strikers angrily screamed at us, banging pots and pans as they shouted. I saw all the ferocity on their sweaty faces. They wanted to hang us for being scabs. In one moment of fear and rage, I wanted to run at them with knives in both hands and hack my way through the crowd. Then again, I loathed myself more than I despised them.

After the first week, the banging and screaming wasn't enough. The strikers wanted to chase us away from manning the door. They began lighting cherry bombs and tossing them at us. The cops didn't stop them; they were on the side of the union strikers.

One morning I arrived, and the mob had already reached a frenzied shriek, like the devil had been let loose.

"You motherfucking scabbie," a tall Hispanic man yelled, as he raced left to right, up and down the street. He was close enough for me to see that his eyes were red. His face was unshaven. Thick black curls matted his head, drenched with perspiration. I looked directly at him as he shouted, but it felt like I was dreaming. I wanted to go to him and apologize and yet I wanted him to stop. I would have bashed his head with a brick to make him stop.

"Don't listen to him," said Virgil.

"I'm trying not to, but I can't not listen to him."

"Just turn away," said Virgil, walking towards an approaching taxi that drove up to the hotel.

Suddenly, out of nowhere, we heard a loud popping sound, then smoke from a cherry bomb exploded a few feet away from us. The guests stepping out of a taxi recoiled in disgust, their hands protecting their faces. I watched the smoke from the explosive curl and twist in the light summer wind. I looked at the cops in the distance, standing near the strikers. They didn't do anything. They turned away. Some had hands in their pockets, some were on walkie-talkies.

"They're going to fucking kill us," I said to Virgil.

"I know," he said. "Just keep moving. If we keep moving, they can't get us."

That day, the strikers threw a few more cherry bombs. Some came very close.

* * *

The next morning, the racket from the crowd picked up shortly after I arrived. The sun was hammering down on all of us, like it was angry. There was something in the air, something sinister.

Then, the cherry bombs started again.

We tried to focus on the tasks, helping people from taxis, taking luggage into the lobby. But we looked over our shoulders and behind each other, worried about a sudden attack. My neck twitched. Meanwhile, the sun poured down in disgust, its rays like burning spikes.

Suddenly, there was another cherry bomb explosion, then a commotion. People had gathered around a cop rolled into a fetal position on the ground. A cherry bomb had blown up in his face. The other cops were scrambling around to help the injured officer. His police cap sat a few feet away from him.

Now the police moved towards the strikers. I couldn't hear what they said. The cops signaled to the strikers that they needed to move back. Suddenly, an ambulance came, its sirens exaggerated and brash, like wounded trumpets. The EMT put the wounded cop on a stretcher, then grabbed the cop's hat and placed it atop his body. The cop was writhing, his hands on his face. I didn't see blood. The sunlight chased the ambulance down the street as it left, the reflecting light violently flickering off its back windows.

That was the last of the cherry bombs.

* * *

A few days passed. The screaming and noise had become normal to us. Virgil and I talked loudly over the crowd when we spoke. It was war. Who was going to get out of this alive?

Then a taxi pulled up, but it wasn't my turn to help the guest. It was Jerome's, the doorman who'd only two days ago replaced the first two doormen who had quit or were fired. There were new doormen hired and fired every day. The hotel needed a stable of about six to eight doormen to cover the three daily shifts.

Jerome walked toward the taxi, opened the door. I could sense there was some hesitation on the part of the guest. Then Jerome nodded in agreement with the guest. He walked towards Virgil and me.

"They said they don't want me. They want you to come over."

"What'd they say?" I asked.

"They didn't say nothing."

I walked over to the cab, opened the door and said, "Can I help you?"

"Yes, take our luggage please. We don't want a nigger touching our bags."

Shocked, I held the door of the cab open and then went to the trunk.

The man and woman emerged from the taxi. They were dressed luxuriantly. The woman was long and slender, wearing slacks and high heels. The man wore sunglasses, his hair was perfectly coiffed, slicked down with grease.

I grabbed their suitcases from the trunk of the taxi and loaded them onto the cart. After I walked the cart over to the bellboy, the man said, "Take this." Pushing up his sunglasses, I saw the blue of his eyes, like miniature paradises. He handed me a handsome tip.

"I'm glad you're standing up against these pieces of shit." He winked, then pushed his sunglasses back down over his eyes. The sun quickly beamed off his glasses, making him impossible to look at. I took the money and walked back to my brother.

"He gave me ten dollars," I said.

"Look at you. You were lucky, you got the Hollywood stars. I got the cheapies," he said, showing me the two dollars and fifty cents he'd received.

"Yeah, but you always make more," I countered, still dazed from the man's words.

"It's the shift," he countered. It wasn't just the shift. Virgil never took a break. He kept going, he kept hustling. I took my allotted fifteen-minute breaks to smoke pot a few blocks down the street. I could do this stoned, maybe. Virgil didn't even take lunch.

Virgil showed me how you could get a five-dollar tip from a cabbie if you directed an airport fare to them. He'd learned it from another doorman. Limo drivers might give you ten dollars if you gave them multiple fares. This would piss off the other cabbies who queued in line to get an airport fare. It backfired on us once.

I directed a guest to one of the cabbies not in queue. As I loaded the luggage in the trunk of the car, I pocketed the five-dollar bill that sat on the carpeted red surface of the trunk. The cab pulled away. One of the drivers who had been in queue pulled in front of the other taxis in line.

The strikers cheered the cab driver's victory.

"Get back in line," I said.

"What are you going to do about it," the driver shot back.

"Fuck you is what I'm going to do about it," I said, banging on the roof of his car.

The crowd clapped. My brother came towards me as the driver got out of the car. He was a lanky African man, maybe two feet taller than me. If we'd all stabbed each other to death, the strikers would have applauded.

"I'll break your fucking face, asshole," I said, almost beside myself with rage. My brother and I stood like two sentries, unmoving. The driver looked at our faces. He knew we were not going to move.

"Tough guy, eh?" said the driver with an accent, now cracking a smile. "You are one tough motherfucker. I won't fuck with you. If you crazy enough to fight these people, who knows what you might do?" he continued, pointing at the strikers, now frenzied, yelling, banging pots and pans. He got back in his car, laughing, and drove away.

We had gained respect among the cab drivers, among the other doormen and even among the strikers. Even if they wanted to kill us, the enmity we achieved was like the respect demons in hell give each other.

* * *

Smoking pot made the days melt into each other. They were connected by screams and sudden roars of the crowd. One night I had a dream that I was driving in a black Cadillac limousine through an empty town. My limo was air-conditioned, but I could see the mix of humidity and sun glare from the car window. In a broken-down wooden house, I saw a door ajar. Driving by, I peered inside and saw a swarm of naked savages attacking each other, some biting, tearing the flesh off others, some dead. As we continued to drive, the car slowed down and was approached by a gang of zombie-like creatures. They clawed at the car, their eyes red and bleary, their teeth long and sharp. Then they smashed the window of the car open and a gush of hot air flooded the interior. The sun was so strong it melted down on the scene like golden snow. In utter fear, I was sweating, my heart thudding. Then I woke up.

* * *

Weeks into the strike now, I had heard that the hotel union was gathering its forces to march up Sixth Avenue. I didn't know how many people would be marching, but I was told there would be many thousands.

"Where do we go when the marchers come?" I asked Virgil.

"We continue to do our job," he said. Being my older brother, Virgil felt he had to calm me and not make my nerves any worse. I know he was afraid, too. I could tell by the look on his face. We'd grown up in a tough neighborhood, standing together, back to back. The difference now was that these weren't street kids, this was the bigger world, the world of unions, of people who had children and full lives.

Later that day, just before Virgil's shift ended, we were told the march was now coming up Sixth Avenue.

"How many people are marching?" Virgil asked.

"Maybe ten thousand," said the Bell Captain, Tommy.

"What are we supposed to do?" Virgil asked for both of us.

"You keep your position, standing at the door."

"We can't leave?"

"No, you can't leave. You took this job," said Tommy. He couldn't care less if we lived or died and he wasn't embarrassed to show it.

About two hours later, we could see a massive crowd of people, some bearing signs, some blowing whistles. The collective sound was thundering, like the earth was breaking open to let a demon serpent devour it. There were thousands upon thousands of people.

"Let us come inside," pleaded my brother, attempting to open the big glass door, leaning his head inside the hotel.

"No, you'll have to stay out there. Besides, you can't leave now," said Tommy, closing the door. He was right. There was nowhere to go.

Now the crowd of marchers were closer to the entrance. To me they looked like one big creature with thousands of tiny heads. They looked like a pink, brown and black worm that was twisting and writhing as they slithered up Sixth Avenue. They weren't walking. They were slicking across the ground, rolling and undulating like a long train of guts.

As they came towards the hotel, the police formed a barricade. Like a virus they pushed against the membrane of the barricade. The police pushed back. The crowd oozed out and shrunk back. There was shouting and cursing. The din was deafening.

Virgil and I didn't speak. We just stood side by side in awe. We didn't hate the people marching. I no longer felt fear. I felt exposed. The mass of guts that slicked up the street wasn't out there; it wasn't something else.

Virgil and I knew that our blood and guts were mixed in that fleshy bloody heap.

SOMETIMES VIVALDI

In my first job out of college, working for an accounting software company, I met Jonathan Rothschild. Jonathan worked in the mailroom.

One Monday I stepped into the mailroom.

"Close the door," he said.

I pointed at myself and looked at the door.

"Yes, please," he added. I closed the door, uncertain as to what would follow.

He began to pace the room, passionately reciting a lengthy excerpt from Kant's *Critique of Pure Reason*, while pressing his thumb to his index and middle finger. It was a nervous tic, as if he spoke a silent duck language that only geniuses understood.

Someone knocked on the office wall.

"Keep it down in there," I heard Alice from accounting shout. Her office was on the other side of wall.

Jonathan began to whisper.

"I'm only interested in the German philosophers: Kant, Wittgenstein and Goethe," said Jonathan, frantically flicking his wrist. He didn't look directly at me when he spoke. He looked at the ground, sometimes twitching his neck. He was short, slightly overweight. He had curly brown hair with tight curls and wore glasses.

"Why only the Germans?" I asked.

"You see, I am a Rothschild," he said. "I come from a long line of intellectual German Jews. My family were bankers, lawyers and scholars in Germany. I was raised on all things German," he added.

He rose up from his seat, gesticulating and reciting Goethe urgently in German.

I put my fingers to my lips saying hush.

Alice pounded on the wall again.

"I'm heading back to my office," I said, concerned that I would be implicated in Jonathan's shenanigans.

"Come back later," said Jonathan. "I want to talk to you about classical music."

I was eager to learn from him. Jonathan was not ordinary in any way. He was completely wild, maybe even brilliant.

At twenty-two, I knew a little about Bach, but wanted to know more about classical music. A few years prior, I had met a girl at a college party. She took me back to her room and we started to make out. She then put music on and turned out the lights. "That's an instrumental Elton John piece?" I asked. "No," she replied, dryly. "That's Beethoven's Moonlight Sonata." I could tell she lost interest in me after that. I knew I had a lot to learn. I vowed to only explore new music. I bought jazz and classical music and sought out people to teach me what they knew about music and music history.

The next day I visited Jonathan again in the mailroom, Bach playing on the radio.

"Do you know what a fugue is?" he asked. I said that I did. I had read Gödel, Escher, Bach in a philosophy class in college. I had then bought cassette tapes of Bach fugues and toccatas. I loved to listen to the patterns in Bach's music, chasing down the voices as they threaded into each other, one voice asserting itself into the foreground, then stepping back into the fray, letting another voice into the foreground.

Jonathan proceeded to lecture me on the history of the fugue. He went on and on in a professorial manner, marching as he spoke, emphasizing his points with both hands upraised, sometimes even shouting.

"I only listen to Bach, Beethoven, Haydn, Handel, Mozart and sometimes Vivaldi," exclaimed Jonathan, after a rambling, but interesting, discussion on fugues. He repeated this phrase over and over for the next year.

"Why sometimes Vivaldi?" I asked.

"Sometimes he's not pure Italian saccharine," he said.

The next day Alice cornered me near the coffee machine. She was only a few years older than me but seemed much more mature.

"Why do you spend so much time with that lunatic Jonathan?" she asked. The diamond on her wedding ring protruded like a small glittering egg.

"I'm interested to learn more about classical music."

"Come to my office in thirty minutes; I can teach you a thing or two about classical music," she demanded, then swiftly spun around and sashayed away.

I knocked on her door as requested thirty minutes later.

"Come in," she said. "And shut the door."

She leaned back and raised the volume on her radio. It was playing classical music. That's maybe Mozart, I thought to myself. I started to guess at the period and the composers of the classical music pieces I heard. I knew it wasn't Elton John.

"I have two tickets to hear Haydn at Lincoln Center if you're interested."

I paused, because she was married.

"Well?" she shouted.

I didn't say anything.

"Are you worried that I'm married?"

I held my gaze at her face. She was pretty, with full thick lips, tanned skin. I had noticed her tight skirts before.

"Don't worry, he's an asshole, my husband. He doesn't know I exist." Her eyes started to water. "He doesn't fuck me, so there's that."

I tried to act cool, but the truth was I was nervous.

She stood up, walked around the desk and reached down my pants, taking my cock in her hand. I had never been approached like that, so I jumped back a bit.

"What do we have here?" Being in my twenties my cock sprung to ready attention, like a soldier with a hot rifle.

"Listen, it'll be classical music and cock play between us, okay?" She spoke to me like Mrs. Taylor, my eighth-grade math teacher.

"There'll be no love, no long walks, no hand-holding."

I nodded agreement.

She then turned to the office door, made sure it was locked and pulled my pants down, kneeling in front of me. She put my cock in her mouth. Her mouth was warm and wet. She expertly sucked until I exploded. All in less than a minute or two.

She stood up, grabbed a tissue from her desk and wiped her mouth.

"Now, take these." She handed me disks of Haydn's music. "Listen to these so you'll follow the concert music."

"Thank you."

"You don't talk much. That's good," she said.

I took the CDs and left her office, floating in the air. I couldn't believe what had just happened.

That weekend we met at Lincoln Center. She looked amazing in her short tight skirt. Her full breasts pushed out from her blouse. She smelled like flowers. I gave her a hug hello. She then kissed me on the lips. I looked around, left and right, hoping that her husband wasn't following us.

She took me by the hand, and we walked into the concert hall.

It was a spectacular show. I could feel the physicality of the cellos and other string instruments, rushing over me like a waterfall. The sounds thudded in my chest and swelled my heart. Alice held my hand the whole time, squeezing it at peak moments in the music.

We walked to Central Park after the concert. It was dark. We sat on a bench and talked about classical music.

"Who are your favorites?" she asked.

"Bach, Beethoven, Haydn, Handel, Mozart and sometimes Vivaldi," I said, feeling like a jerk after I opened my mouth.

"You sound like that robot Jonathan now. Why don't you just listen to a car engine?" Then she smiled. "I'm teasing you." She stroked my leg. "I like the Italians best. I love the passion. I love opera. If I want to listen to a clock tick, I listen to Bach." I was getting aroused. Then she leaned into me, giving me open-mouth kisses, covering my mouth with her lips, as if she was pulling me into a centrifuge. She unzipped my pants and jerked me off, finishing with her mouth.

I walked her to a cab, while we held hands.

"I had a terrific night," she said.

"I did too."

That Monday I saw Alice at the coffee machine. She was cordial but formal. After filling her cup, she raised her eyebrows, saying that she needed to speak to me about some invoices later.

After lunch I strolled by the mailroom.

"May I come in?" I asked.

"Yes, yes," said Jonathan. Then pointing at one of his mailroom colleagues he said, "I was just speaking to Bob here about Bach's Cello Suites, but he's too much of a troglodyte to understand."

"You know Jonathan, payroll is going to be late today," said Bob.

"No, today is payday," replied Jonathan.

"Not today. The system was down," said Bob, snickering, trying to make Jonathan blow his top.

Jonathan then stood up and began pacing back and forth, making an uproar. "Today is payday I have to get paid today. Not tomorrow. Today."

Bob kept saying "No check today," making the situation worse. Then Bob left the mailroom. Jonathan was practically bouncing off the ceiling, pounding his fists on the walls and his desk, repeating, "Got to get the paycheck today."

"Jonathan, listen to me," I said. But he kept repeating himself, talking over me.

"If I don't get the check, I can't pay my rent."

"Jonathan, Bob is teasing you."

"I need the paycheck."

"I know you do. I think he was just teasing you for calling him a troglodyte."

"But he is a troglodyte."

"No one likes to be called that."

We spoke like this for a while, going around and round. He calmed down eventually, then walked over to the radio and turned up the volume.

"Ah, yes, Bach, Beethoven, Haydn, Handel, Mozart," he said.

"And sometimes Vivaldi," I added.

"Yes, sometimes."

Over the next few months, things were up and down with Alice. I followed her lead. If she called me to talk dirty to me on the phone at my desk, I went along. I came to her when she called me into her office. If she ignored me, that was okay too. We had sex in the bathroom at work. She gave me head in the stairwell—more than once. We went to several concerts. And for my birthday, she bought me *Pavarotti Sings Puccini*.

But she then stopped calling me into her office. Then all at once, she began ignoring me all the time. Had I done something? Then one day I saw that she was pregnant. It wasn't mine. I assumed things were now going well for her at home. While I was happy for her and somewhat relieved, I also felt a sting in my stomach. Our little game was over. But whatever alchemy she had wrought to fix her marriage had maybe worked. I didn't know.

Now I could identify Mozart pretty much all the time, only confusing his concertos with Beethoven's—sometimes. I had developed a decent catalogue of classical music. And whatever craziness the year had brought, it was now past.

PIRATE JESUS

"Before you sit down," my mother says, "go to Happy's Liquor to get wine." Reaching in her purse, she holds out a twenty-dollar bill.

"I'll get it for you," I say.

"Don't you do that to me," she says, holding the bill like a spike.

I'm visiting my mom with my girlfriend, Susan. My mom lives in the Queensview co-operative complex, across the street from the Ravenswood projects where I grew up.

"That's okay, I got it."

"No, take it," she says, shoving the money in my hand. It's easier for me to take the twenty dollars than argue with her. My mother's eyes look gigantic behind her glasses. At five foot two, she can roar like a volcano.

Susan comes with me to the store; she's too uncomfortable to stay alone with my mother. My mother is like a human heart with its flesh exposed to the air. Susan is secret and sullen like a caterpillar in its chrysalis. She might not kiss me in front of my family, but she'll demand that I fuck her in the bathroom of a bar.

We walk to Happy's on the projects' side of the street. The clerk and merchandise are protected by a thick plexiglass panel. I slide my mother's twenty through the slot between the window slats. The clerk takes the money and hands me the bottle of wine.

Leaving Happy's, Susan and I walk down to the projects building where I grew up. I tell Susan that I want to take her to the roof.

"This isn't some plot of yours is it?" she asks.

"You can trust me," I say. To get to the roof we have to take the elevator to the sixth floor then walk up to the landing below the roof exit door. The roof door is ajar, just the way I left it years ago. The wind makes the door bang like a tin can.

As we walk out onto the roof I say, "See, look at this," sweeping my hand over the view of Manhattan. Atop the piss-ridden hallways and gray stone stairwells, the sun's rays make the silver towers sparkle as if on fire across the Hudson.

I come up behind Susan as she gazes at Manhattan. Her head moves from left to right, looking at the island from Downtown to Harlem.

I wrap my arms around her, kissing her neck.

"This is beautiful," she says. I love the way she lisps slightly when she talks. She speaks clearly, enunciating every word. She's not like the girls I grew up with, the girls that fooled around with me on this roof so many years ago. Susan studied feminism and art in college. Most of the people I grew up with didn't go to college.

I press my groin into her.

"It's beautiful, but this isn't my idea of romantic. Don't think you're getting anything."

"But this would be perfect. No one would see us if we messed around up here."

"I'll make up for it when we get home," she says holding me tight, then pushing me away.

I walk her to the different corners of the roof. I explain how Lan and I used to jump the fence to the next building. This enabled us to then walk down the stairs of the adjoining building for a quick escape. I almost fell off the roof once.

Then I remember that the purpose of this visit is to see my mother and I still have to bring her the wine.

We take the ride down the elevator; it shakes and rattles like a broken-down train. The sounds echo in the elevator chamber and are then swallowed up into its walls.

Leaving the project building, we bump into Junior, an old friend from the neighborhood. Junior was in a gang called "The Hated Ones." The Hated Ones hung out near Happy's drinking beer, smoking pot and starting fights. They wore dungaree jackets with The Hated Ones logo on it. Sometimes they stole beer from the Korean deli up the street from Happy's. They might have stabbed others and got stabbed, but they never killed anyone.

The last time I'd seen Junior, about ten years earlier, he was walking down the street, staggering, with a forty-ounce bottle of Olde English. I knew from his swaying, his eyes bulbous but straining to stay open, that he was stoned on crack. He begged me for money. Like an Old Testament prophet, he repeated, "Take me to the promised land," over and over, tightening the red bandana he wore around his forehead, his hand extended, and his eyeballs sucked up into his skull.

I gave him five bucks just to get rid of him.

Junior always wore a bandana. When he was younger, his legs and arms were muscular from running track. He played handball in the park, his stomach drenched in sweat, boasting a grill of muscles.

Before Junior started wearing a thick black leather jacket, a leather cap and black motorcycle boots with silver rings, no one could run faster than Junior.

Before his face hardened, his eyebrows arched when he smiled. After eighth grade, Junior's shoulders grew broad. His hands became large like dumbbells. His jaw, once rounder and softer, now was sharper-edged, like an axe blade.

Now when I see Junior about ten feet ahead of me, I look away. I don't want to talk to him high on crack. Junk makes a person no longer themselves. They don't know who you are, or only remember you as if from a dream.

He sees me.

Junior is wearing clean dungaree pants with cuffs. The pants are ironed. He's walking straight, his face is shaved, and his close-cropped Afro is slightly gray.

"Hey Vinny, yo man, how you been?"

He pulls me into him to embrace. His musky perfume smells like bug-spray. A wave of shame overtakes me for wanting to avoid him.

"Junior, how you doing? This is my girlfriend Susan," I say, gesturing towards her, not wanting to shut her out from the conversation. Being from Long Island, Susan has probably never talked to someone from the projects.

"I am doing fine now." Junior points to his chest, skull rings on his bulging knuckles. "But I was in bad shape, bro. Yo, I was inside for five years. But when I was inside, I cleaned up." Looking at my hair, he says, "Man, you fucking gray. But you look good. You must be doing something right with that gray hair to get a pretty girl."

I look at Susan. She winks at me.

"I'm doing good, you know, working," I say, shrugging. I don't talk about my work. I'm embarrassed that I work a suit job.

"This is a good man," says Junior to Susan, patting my arm.

Twenty years ago, I had been the kid high on pot, hanging out on the corner with The Hated Ones. I wasn't a member, but I knew them all. Twenty years ago, my eyes were red most nights as I wasted time standing around in the streets.

Like most people from the neighborhood, Junior speaks in the moment.

"I'm clean now. I found Jesus when I was inside."

I don't look away from his hard stare. "Inside ain't like out here. Anything can happen to motherfuckers," he says. His eyes fill with water.

I'm listening, my eyes follow his hands.

"I fucked up. I robbed people, I stole money," he says. "I don't know what I was doing back then. I hanged with some bad motherfuckers, doing bad shit."

Not knowing what his world was like, I press my lips together, sigh and shake my head.

"But you're okay now," I say.

"When I was inside, I converted to Judaism, but, you know, I was saved by Jesus," says Junior showing me a black ring with a silver Star of David on it. I hold the ring finger and look at it.

"Jesus saved my life man," he says, his face serious. "Motherfucker was ready to die for nothing like a nigger crackhead," he says, wiping tears from his eyes.

I put my hand on his shoulder.

"Have you seen Ness?" I ask, changing the subject, wanting to comfort him. Ness was one of The Hated Ones.

Still drying his face, smiling, he says, "Ness is a doorman in Manhattan now. He's fucking fat, bro. You'd never recognize him."

I try to imagine a fat Ness. Ness was his tag name. Ness climbed up subway walls to scrawl his name. He would have to have been upside-down, one hand holding him from death as he tagged his name. None of his tags remain.

"Remember that fucker, Jimmy Gestapo? Jimmy Schumacher?" asks Junior.

"Gestapo wore a Nazi helmet, talking shit about Hitler."

The summer sun beats down on the project cement and makes our eyes squint in the glare off Junior's golden tooth.

"I used to tell Gestapo to watch out with the racist shit, man" says Junior. "We was Puerto Ricans and niggas in our building."

I laugh and don't say anything.

"He's wack now, in and out of jail, crackhead and shit. See him sometimes when I come to visit my mom in the Bronx where I live."

We talk for a bit more. I am shaken by his honesty. I am proud to come from these people. He doesn't hide behind his skin; he is pure and open.

"Junior, it was great seeing you, man. You look great," I say in a hushed voice.

"You too. You look good. Say hi to your brother for me."

Clasping hands, we draw into each other again, embracing. "He's a good man," pointing to me, says Junior to Susan. "He's a good man."

ACKNOWLEDGMENTS

Thank you to Lan & Joe; our childhood at least gave us some good stories and lifelong friendships. To my family, I appreciate your believing in me when I didn't believe in myself. I'll return the money someday. To fellow writers, Annie Lanzillotto, George Guida, Joanna Claps Herman, Ed Giunta, Steven Cerulli, and Angela Mitchell, I'll never forget your being there when I asked. Susan Kaessinger, Angela Welch, and Bill Bernthal, I appreciate your eyes and hearts. To my constant friend and supporter, Michelle Messina Reale, you've inspired me to reach for the skies. And finally, thank you to Nic Grosso for your efforts and patience in reviewing and editing the manuscript. Of course, all of this is made possible by my wife, Arielle. Without love, nothing makes sense.

ABOUT THE AUTHOR

MIKE FIORITO is currently an Associate Editor for Mad Swirl Magazine and a regular contributor to the Red Hook Star Revue.

The Hated Ones is his fifth book.

His other books include *Falling from Trees, Call Me Guido, Freud's Haberdashery Habits* and *Hallucinating Huxley.*

Mike lives in Brooklyn with his wife and two boys.

VIA Folios

A refereed book series dedicated to the culture of Italians and Italian Americans.

MICHAEL PARENTI. *Waiting for Yesterday: Pages from a Street Kid's Life*. Vol 90. Memoir.

ANNIE LANZILLOTTO. *Schistsong*. Vol 89. Poetry.

EMANUEL DI PASQUALE. *Love Lines*. Vol 88. Poetry.

CAROSONE & LOGIUDICE. *Our Naked Lives*. Vol 87. Essays.

JAMES PERICONI. *Strangers in a Strange Land: A Survey of Italian-Language American Books*. Vol 86. Book History.

DANIELA GIOSEFFI. *Escaping La Vita Della Cucina*. Vol 85. Essays.

MARIA FAMÀ. *Mystics in the Family*. Vol 84. Poetry.

ROSSANA DEL ZIO. *From Bread and Tomatoes to Zuppa di Pesce "Ciambotto"*. Vol. 83. Memoir.

LORENZO DELBOCA. *Polentoni*. Vol 82. Italian Studies.

SAMUEL GHELLI. *A Reference Grammar*. Vol 81. Italian Language.

ROSS TALARICO. *Sled Run*. Vol 80. Fiction.

FRED MISURELLA. *Only Sons*. Vol 79. Fiction.

FRANK LENTRICCHIA. *The Portable Lentricchia*. Vol 78. Fiction.

RICHARD VETERE. *The Other Colors in a Snow Storm*. Vol 77. Poetry.

GARIBALDI LAPOLLA. *Fire in the Flesh*. Vol 76 Fiction & Criticism.

GEORGE GUIDA. *The Pope Stories*. Vol 75 Prose.

ROBERT VISCUSI. *Ellis Island*. Vol 74. Poetry.

ELENA GIANINI BELOTTI. *The Bitter Taste of Strangers Bread*. Vol 73. Fiction.

PINO APRILE. *Terroni*. Vol 72. Italian Studies.

EMANUEL DI PASQUALE. *Harvest*. Vol 71. Poetry.

ROBERT ZWEIG. *Return to Naples*. Vol 70. Memoir.

AIROS & CAPPELLI. *Guido*. Vol 69. Italian/American Studies.

FRED GARDAPHÉ. *Moustache Pete is Dead! Long Live Moustache Pete!*. Vol 67. Literature/Oral History.

PAOLO RUFFILLI. *Dark Room/Camera oscura*. Vol 66. Poetry.

HELEN BAROLINI. *Crossing the Alps*. Vol 65. Fiction.

COSMO FERRARA. *Profiles of Italian Americans*. Vol 64. Italian Americana.

GIL FAGIANI. *Chianti in Connecticut*. Vol 63. Poetry.

BASSETTI & D'ACQUINO. *Italic Lessons*. Vol 62. Italian/American Studies.

CAVALIERI & PASCARELLI, Eds. *The Poet's Cookbook*. Vol 61. Poetry/Recipes.

CPSIA information can be obtained
at www.ICGtesting.com
Printed in the USA
BVHW031033020821
612962BV00002BB/155